"You did read the proposal from the committee, did you not?" Penelope asked.

"I am afraid there has been some mistake," Mr. McGregor said. "I did not ask you here to discuss the stargazing society. You were invited here to discuss the letter you sent to the duke. The letter in which you proposed yourself as a candidate for marriage."

Penelope swallowed hard. "Marriage?"

"Yes."

Suddenly she remembered precisely who the Duke of Torringford was, and why his name had sounded so familiar. She gulped again, as she realized the impossible muddle that she had landed in.

"I assure you, I penned no such note," she said tersely. She rose to her feet, preparing to end the interview.

There was a faint click, and then the sound of the door opening behind her.

"Your Grace, we have been expecting you." Mr. McGregor rose to his feet.

"No, we have not," Penelope said. She turned to face the newcomer.

She had her second surprise of the day. Based on the discussions at the dinner party, Penelope had assumed the new duke was a corpulent lecher, so elderly or repulsive that he could have no hope of winning a bride on his own merits. Nothing could have been further from the truth. The Duke of Torringford was a well-built man, perhaps in his late twenties, with dark brown hair and brown eyes. His plainly tailored blue jacket and tan pants revealed a powerful body, while his sun-browned complexion showed a man used to country life.

She wondered what Harriet Lawton would have thought, had the solicitor summoned her instead.

BOOK YOUR PLACE ON OUR WEBSITE AND MAKE THE READING CONNECTION!

We've created a customized website just for our very special readers, where you can get the inside scoop on everything that's going on with Zebra, Pinnacle and Kensington books.

When you come online, you'll have the exciting opportunity to:

- View covers of upcoming books
- Read sample chapters
- Learn about our future publishing schedule (listed by publication month *and author*)
- Find out when your favorite authors will be visiting a city near you
- Search for and order backlist books from our online catalog
- Check out author bios and background information
- Send e-mail to your favorite authors
- Meet the Kensington staff online
- Join us in weekly chats with authors, readers and other guests
- Get writing guidelines
- AND MUCH MORE!

**Visit our website at
http://www.kensingtonbooks.com**

A MOST SUITABLE DUTCHESS

PATRICIA BRAY

ZEBRA BOOKS
Kensington Publishing Corp.
http://www.kensingtonbooks.com

ZEBRA BOOKS are published by

Kensington Publishing Corp.
850 Third Avenue
New York, NY 10022

All Kensington titles, imprints, and distributed lines are
available at special quantity discounts for bulk purchases for
sales promotion, premiums, fund-raising, educational or in-
stitutional use.

Special book excerpts or customized printings can also be
created to fit specific needs. For details, write or phone the
office of the Kensington Special Sales Manager: Kensington
Publishing Corp., 850 Third Avenue, New York, NY 10022.
Attn. Special Sales Department. Phone: 1-800-221-2647.

Zebra and the Z logo Reg. U.S. Pat. & TM Off.

First Printing: December 2001
10 9 8 7 6 5 4 3 2 1

Printed in the United States of America

ONE

"Your Grace?"

Marcus Heywood heard the voice, but continued his perusal of the newspaper. An article on the proposed agricultural reform laws had caught his eye, but he shook his head in disbelief as he read on. Hadn't those fools in Parliament done enough harm already with their ill-advised tariffs and agricultural reform laws? The solution was fewer restrictive laws, not more. Any landholder would tell them the same.

"Your Grace?" the voice repeated, a trifle more loudly.

Marcus looked up at the man, and then glanced around at the room. Save for himself and the clerk, the small antechamber was empty. He flushed as he realized the clerk was speaking to him.

The clerk caught his eye. "Your Grace, Mr. Forsythe has returned and will see you now."

Marcus rose, hastily discarding the newspaper, and hoped that he did not look as foolish as he felt. Your Grace. He could not get used to the new mode of address. For the past month he had half expected that he would wake up, and discover that this had all been a bizarre dream. But now the truth was beginning to sink in, and with it the realization that he was indeed the new Duke of Torringford.

The clerk led him down a short hall, then opened a door, and bowed him through.

"His Grace, the Duke of Torringford," the clerk announced.

Marcus winced.

A middle-aged gentleman rose from his seat behind a mahogany desk, and bowed. "Your Grace, it is an honor to make your acquaintance, despite these regrettable circumstances. May I offer you my condolences on the death of your cousin, the former duke?"

"I am pleased to make your acquaintance as well," Marcus said. "And as for the duke, he was a distant cousin indeed. I am certain you knew him far better than I."

Marcus would not pretend to any great sorrow. Indeed, he had encountered the former Duke of Torringford only twice in his life. The first time had been at a cousin's wedding, the second time at the Newmarket races. Neither encounter had been particularly memorable. The gulf between the great duke and his distant country cousins had been too wide, and neither side had the least inclination to attempt to bridge the gap.

Marcus took a seat, and then Mr. Forsythe resumed his own seat behind the desk. He withdrew a handkerchief from his pocket, and began to mop his forehead.

"Your message indicated some matter of great urgency?" Marcus prompted.

"Indeed," the solicitor said, his double chins wobbling as he nodded his head vigorously. "A matter of some urgency, and discretion, which is why I wished to speak with you myself."

A month ago, Marcus had been at Greenfields, supervising the spring planting. The solicitor's letter informing him that he was the new Duke of Torringford had seemed a strange jest. He had felt no urgency in following up on the matter. His inheritance could wait, the spring planting could not.

The solicitor's second letter had been more forceful, requesting his presence in Edinburgh as soon as possible. Marcus had ignored that, too, not yet ready to face his changed circumstances. But the third letter had insisted that he come at once, hinting at dire consequences should he fail to appear.

"In his final years, the duke was much burdened by his losses. It was common knowledge that he was increasingly concerned about securing the succession, and that the traditions of Torringford would be carried on after his death."

Marcus nodded. "He had more than his share of misfortunes," he said.

The old duke had had six sons, which should have been enough for any man. One had died in infancy, but five had survived to adulthood. The succession should have been well secured. But the oldest had died of a fever, and another had died in the colonial war. Two had married late in life, and died childless. Only the youngest had married and produced a son of his own.

"You must understand that the duke was, er, concerned when he realized his grandson George Wallace was to inherit the title."

Concerned. More likely the old duke had been furious when he realized his title was to fall to such a wastrel.

George Wallace was only two years Marcus's junior, the same age as his brother Reginald. The three of them had briefly been at school together, before George found himself expelled from Oxbridge, as he had been expelled from so many other schools before.

Even then, George had made himself unpopular, insisting that the other boys treat him with the deference due a future duke, alternating between promising great favors or making dire threats, all to be fulfilled when he came into his title. Marcus, like most of his friends, had found George insufferable, and had avoided his company. It seemed time had done little to change George Wallace's character.

And all George's promises had come to naught, for he had been killed this spring in a coaching accident. If he had lived another month he would have been the new duke, but instead that title had landed on Marcus's most unlikely shoulders.

"May I ask when you were born?"

"June. June the sixth."

"And the year?"

"I fail to see what this has to do . . ."

"Please indulge me."

"Seventeen hundred and eighty-five." In less than a month he would turn thirty.

"Good, there is still time."

"What do you mean?"

"Last year the duke rewrote his will. The original ducal estate is entailed, but the rest of his properties and personal fortune were not, and their disposition was at his discretion."

The solicitor's eyes met his, and then looked away. His nervousness was plain to read. So the duke's fortune was not entailed, was it? No doubt the solicitor feared telling him that the duke had decided to leave it all to a former mistress, or perhaps the son of an old friend. Anything, rather than risk seeing it fall into the hands of George Wallace.

No doubt Mr. Forsythe expected that Marcus would be angry, but instead he felt relieved. He had never wanted a grand title, or the responsibilities that came with the possession of great wealth. He had seen this inheritance as a burden, and would be well pleased to find out that the burden had passed to another.

"And how did he choose to dispose of his wealth?" Marcus asked softly.

Mr. Forsythe clasped his hands together. "The will is written so that the fortune passes to the next

Duke of Torringford, provided that he is married by the time he reaches his thirtieth birthday."

Marcus stared at the fire, a half-filled brandy glass in his hand, while Mrs. Porter cleared away the remains of their dinner. At least Reginald had done justice to the excellent pheasant, but his own plates were largely untouched. Once, the innkeeper's wife would have clucked at him over such behavior, urging him to eat a proper meal, but now she confined herself to a mere frown.

"Will there be aught else, Your Worships?" Mrs. Porter asked.

"No. Thank you, Mrs. Porter," he said, rousing himself from his reverie.

She gave a half curtsy and departed.

Reginald rose from the table, bringing with him the brandy decanter. He refilled his brother's glass and then his own, before taking a seat in the chair opposite Marcus.

"You scarcely said three words at dinner," Reginald began. "And you never did answer my questions about your visit to the solicitor."

Marcus lifted his gaze to his brother's face, taking comfort in the honest concern he read there. At least Reginald still regarded him as he always had.

"Your Worships," he repeated with a grim chuckle. "Even the Porters stand on ceremony with me now. Me, whom they have known for twenty years, ever since Father first brought me to

Edinburgh. Yet now it is as if I am a stranger to them."

Reginald shrugged. "What did you expect? Noblemen are scarce in this quarter, and I'll wager they have never played host to a duke. Once the novelty wears off, they will resume their old ways."

"I suppose," he said. But inside he was not so certain. Becoming a peer of the realm was not something he could lightly set aside. He feared very much that his days of quiet living and unpretentiousness were over.

The solicitor Forsythe, the law clerk, the Porters, even his neighbors and acquaintances all seemed to expect him to behave differently, now that he was a duke. And yet inside he felt no different. He had not changed. It was they who had changed, or rather, who had changed their expectations of him.

It was as if he were no longer a man, but rather a thing. A ducal title made of flesh. It made him uneasy, but he knew it was not the real reason for his despondency. He was focusing on trifles, because he did not want to think about the solicitor's unwelcome revelations.

But he could play coward no longer. It was time to tell his brother the truth.

He took a sip of the imported French brandy, barely tasting it. Which was a shame, as he suspected Mr. Porter had gone to some trouble to acquire a beverage worthy of his ducal guest.

"It seems our late cousin altered his will once he learned George Wallace was to inherit. He wished to encourage George to mend his reckless ways, and to carry on the line," Marcus began.

"And?" Reginald prompted.

"He could do nothing about the title, or the entailed property. But his personal fortune, and the majority of the estates, will pass to the heir only if he is married by his thirtieth birthday."

"Damn," Reginald said softly.

"Indeed," Marcus agreed.

There was a moment of silence.

"I assume you told the solicitor to go hang? You don't need the money, after all. And you were never one to let anyone else dictate your course."

His brother knew him well.

"I would have, but there is a problem. It seems that George borrowed heavily against his expectations. Debts that I am honor-bound to discharge." He took another sip of brandy. "Over a hundred thousand pounds, actually."

Reginald gulped his own brandy, and swallowed hard. "What fool would lend such a sum to a rakehell like George?"

"Does it matter?"

His brother shook his head.

"There is no way to pay them, of course," Marcus said. "Even if I sold Greenfields, the hounds, everything I own, it would still not serve."

And to think that only a month ago he had thought himself a prosperous gentleman, master of Greenfields, and the five thousand a year that it brought in under his management. Yet George Wallace had gambled away twenty times such a sum. He could not imagine how anyone could be so reckless.

"So what will you do?"

"Marry," Marcus said, giving a bitter laugh. "What else can I do? I had Forsythe send the will over to McGregor, but I expect he will confirm that all is in order."

Mr. Forsythe had been furious when he realized that Marcus wanted his own solicitor to review the misbegotten will. No doubt his anger owed less to the implied slur on his competence than it did to the realization that his firm was unlikely to continue its lucrative relationship with the new Duke of Torringford.

"Have you a bride in mind? Or did the solicitor have one picked out for you?" Reginald asked.

"Alice Dunne will do as well as any other," Marcus said, without any real enthusiasm. Alice was an amiable woman, but he had never felt any romantic attraction to her, or to any of her younger sisters for that matter. Still she came from good stock, and their families had been neighbors for decades.

Alice had never shown him any sign of partiality before, treating him with the same affectionate friendship that she showed toward Reginald and the other gentlemen of the county. And yet, at the age of three-and-twenty her prospects for marriage were dwindling. Perhaps she would be grateful for this chance.

"Alice is a fine girl," Reginald said. "But somehow I never pictured her as a duchess."

"Nor myself as a duke," Marcus countered. "We will both have to grow into our roles."

"I am sorry," Reginald said, reaching over to grasp his forearm.

Marcus nodded, grateful beyond measure for his brother's sympathy. He knew few others would share it. Most would count him lucky. Even after paying off George Wallace's debts, he would still be extremely wealthy, with a title that ensured him entry to the highest levels of society. And Miss Alice Dunne would make a good wife. Of course she would.

They sat in companionable silence, moving only to refill their glasses or to add another log to the fire when it burned low.

"What you really need is a nobleman's daughter," Reginald said suddenly, interrupting his train of thought. "Someone bred to the role of great lady, comfortable in society and able to manage a grand household. A wife like that could show you the way to go on."

"And where do you suggest I find such a paragon? Remember, I have less than a month to find her, woo her, and wed her."

"Advertise. As you would for a prize broodmare, or the new kennel master," Reginald suggested.

His brother rose and crossed over to the writing desk that occupied the corner of the sitting room. Lifting the top, he withdrew a piece of parchment, and then sorted through the quills till he found one to his satisfaction.

Marcus watched in bemusement as Reginald hastily scribbled a few lines.

"How does this sound? 'Seeking young, unattached gentlewoman of excellent breeding and character, for position as Duchess of Torringford. Candidate must be experienced in household management. Serious inquires only.' "

Marcus grinned. "And what about her appearance? Shall you condemn me to marriage with a hag?"

"Very well," Reginald said. "I'll add 'comely' to the list of virtues."

" 'Intelligent' and 'well spoken,' would be nice. I might as well be particular in my requirements."

"Of course. You are a duke now, after all," Reginald said.

They looked at each other and began to laugh, soft chuckles that grew into full-throated laughter, as the absurdity of the situation struck them anew. It was better to laugh than to despair.

"A shame that matters are not so simple," Marcus said, when he finally caught his breath.

"When was life ever simple?" Reginald asked, a slight slur to his words.

Marcus was aware that they had both had more to drink than was wise. Especially him, for he needed to make an early start on the morrow.

"I will retire now. It is an early start for me," Marcus said.

"To Greenfields?"

"Yes, and then to see Mr. Dunne and ask for his daughter's hand."

"I will come with you," Reginald said.

"No," Marcus said swiftly. He loved his brother, but did not want his company. This was something he had to do alone. "I need you to stay here. Make certain the notice is sent to the *Gazette*, asking all interested in the position of kennel master to send their particulars to McGregor. You can interview them and make your choice."

"Me?"

"Who else? You will have to manage Greenfields in my absence, and show the new master his duties. I am afraid I will be kept busy. There are the duke's properties to be inspected, and no doubt Alice will expect a wedding trip."

He swallowed dryly at that last thought. Just what would Alice expect from him?

"Stay here a week, as we had planned," Marcus said. "Enjoy yourself. By the time you return to Greenfields we will have made arrangements for the wedding."

He was fortunate indeed that he lived in Scotland. In England such a hasty wedding would have required a special license or a mad dash for Gretna Green, or one of the other Scottish border towns.

Here in Scotland the old marriage laws still held. All Marcus and his intended had to do was declare the fact of their marriage in the presence of witnesses. For that their families would be more than sufficient. And then he and his new bride would journey to Edinburgh, and complete the formalities necessary to secure his inheritance.

"Marcus, if there is anything I can do—"

"I know," Marcus said. "Thank you. But this is something only I can do."

TWO

The pages of the *Edinburgh Courant* crackled as James Hastings turned them. "Lackwitted fool," he muttered as some article caught his eye.

Penelope Hastings gazed at her older brother and bit back a sigh. James was in a foul mood this morning. She had known it from the moment he joined her in the dining room, giving her only a curt greeting before turning his attention to his tea and the newspapers laid next to his plate.

Accustomed to her brother's moods, she had ignored his incivility, and had instead calmly taken her own repast, enjoying the hearty porridge and freshly made scones. Now as she sipped her chocolate, she wondered whether she should leave her brother in peace or try to discover what was troubling him.

"I thought I might visit the shops today," Penelope said. "We need new linens, and if they are not too dear, perhaps new drapes for the sitting room."

James made no response.

"While I am out, are there any commissions I can execute for you?" Penelope asked.

"No," James said, his attention seemingly fixed on his newspaper. Yet he had been reading the same page for the last several minutes. Surely the *Edinburgh Courant* contained no news that would hold his interest so closely. He was simply using the newspaper to avoid speaking with her.

He was deliberately trying to aggravate her, but she knew him too well to fall for such a transparent ploy.

"Remember this evening I am to dine with the Lawtons. And then we are to go hear Mr. Creighton's lecture on the latest astronomical discoveries. I believe this month he will be discussing comets. Will you be joining us?" she asked.

The newspaper was folded with a snap of his wrists, and laid on the table with far more force than was necessary.

"No, I will not be joining you," he said, meeting her gaze for the first time this morning.

Ah. A reaction at last.

"Very well, I will convey your regards to the Lawtons," she said.

"I will be escorting Miss Carstairs to a musicale this evening," James said. "You might wish to consider joining us instead. So you can make your apologies."

"Apologies?"

"Certainly. Miss Carstairs told me all about the literary salon the other day. How she was humiliated and how you did nothing to defend her. I could not believe my own sister capable of such rudeness."

Now she knew what had prompted his earlier pique.

"I regret that she did not enjoy herself," Penelope said carefully, forbearing to mention that it had been his idea that she invite Miss Carstairs. "The members of the literary society enjoy lively debate, it is true, but it is a civilized discourse."

"Amelia told me they laughed at her," James said, for once breaking from his careful formality.

Had they? She could not remember, but in truth she had been too busy playing hostess, moving from one cluster of friends to another, to pay particular attention to Miss Carstairs. Perhaps she should have watched over her more closely.

"I am certain they did not mean to be unkind," she said. And yet she wondered. The members of the literary society would not be deliberately rude. But they had little patience for fools.

"And you were rude to her as well," James said.

"I merely suggested that she actually read *Waverly*, before she ventured to give an opinion on the novel, or on the identity of its author."

Indeed the topic of that afternoon had been a lively debate on whether or not Sir Walter Scott was indeed the author of *Waverly*. Penelope and others had argued for this premise, noting similarities in the lyrical prose of the novel to Scott's poetic works.

When asked her opinion, Miss Carstairs had made the mistake of saying that she had never read the novel, but she was certain that a great poet would never lower himself so far as to write a mere romantic novel. Her ignorant remark had been received with polite disbelief.

Rather than arguing her case, as any other member of the society would, Miss Carstairs had wilted and soon made her excuses to leave.

"So now you blame Miss Carstairs?"

Her brother seemed determined to pick a fight with her, despite her own good intentions.

"If Miss Carstairs feels she was slighted, then I will make my apologies to her. Naturally she is welcome to join us for the next meeting, but I think it would be wise if she did not. Such gatherings are not to everyone's taste."

"You will apologize," James said gravely, as if he were her father and not merely her elder brother. "And the literary society is no longer welcome to meet here. You will have to make other arrangements."

"What?" He could not mean this.

"This is to be Miss Carstairs's home one day, if she will have me. And I will not have her feel unwelcome in her own house," James said. His face had that stubborn expression that reminded her of a willful child, intent on getting his own way.

A thousand angry words sprang to mind, and she bit her lip to keep them from escaping. How dare James criticize her manners, dismissing her as if she were the interloper here. Penelope rose from the table, intent on making her retreat before she said something she would forever regret.

As she passed by her brother's seat, she paused and laid one hand on his shoulder.

"We have always rubbed on well together, haven't we, James?" she asked.

Indeed, in the three years since the death of their mother, they had settled into a comfortable routine. Penelope had taken the reins of the household, and James occupied himself with his business affairs and his clubs. While not precisely happy, she had been content. She saw no reason why this should change.

"All things change," James said, as if he read her thoughts.

Indeed she should have seen this coming. More fool that she had not, for his attentions to Miss Carstairs had been marked. And now it was clear that he intended to make her an offer, one which Miss Carstairs would no doubt accept, after the required ladylike demurs.

Then where would she be? Keeping house for her unattached brother was one thing. Living as the dependent of James and his young bride would be another matter entirely, especially since it was clear that Miss Amelia Carstairs bore her no goodwill.

And yet where else could she go? She was barely one-and-twenty, far too young to set up her own household. And marriage was out of the question. She had once known true love, and though Stephen Wolcott was lost to her, she knew she could never find a man to be his equal. And she had vowed never to marry for mere convenience. No matter how difficult she found living with the insufferable Miss Carstairs.

Perhaps when she was firmly on the shelf, she would be able to use her modest inheritance to hire a companion and set up her own household in Edinburgh. In the meantime, she would have to resign herself to making the best of her situation. She had endured the loss of her love, and the deaths of her beloved parents. Surely coping with her brother's marriage was a far lesser challenge. Everything would work out for the best. It simply must, for she had no other choice.

That evening she made her way to the Lawtons' residence in Old Town. The Lawtons had been friends of her mother. Of an age with their youngest daughter Harriet, Penelope had always been treated more as a daughter than as a family friend, and tonight was no exception. She was welcomed warmly, her gown admired, and then admonished to enjoy herself.

She joined the rest of the guests in the drawing room. It was a small party, merely a dozen guests besides herself and the Lawtons. Like herself, those present were patrons of the Royal Astronomical Society, and shared an interest in scientific matters.

Harriet Lawton was chatting with Mr. Ian MacLeod, her auburn curls bouncing as she nodded vigorously in agreement with whatever point the barrister was making. Then she caught sight of Penelope, and waved her over.

"A pleasure to see you this evening, Miss Hastings," Mr. Ian MacLeod said. He was a pleasant enough fellow, although given to a certain portliness.

"The pleasure is mine," Penelope replied. "And, Harriet, I trust I find you and your family well?"

"Yes, yes," Harriet said, clearly out of patience with the social niceties. "But you will never guess what Mr. MacLeod and I were discussing."

"In that case, I pray that you enlighten me," Penelope replied.

Mr. MacLeod rocked back on his heels, crossing his hands across his ample waist. "Miss Lawton and I were discussing the Duke of Torringford."

Penelope wrinkled her brow, unable to place the name. While solidly of the gentry, neither she nor the Lawtons mixed with the aristocratic set. "I do not recall the name. Is he perhaps a new subscriber to the Royal Astronomical Society?"

Harriet giggled. "No, of course not. It is the scandal. Because of the advertisement."

"What advertisement?" Penelope asked

"Did you not see it? It was in this morning's *Advertiser,*" Harriet said.

"And in this afternoon's *Gazette,*" Mr. MacLeod added, not to be outdone.

"I have not seen either," Penelope replied.

"It is most shocking," Harriet said. She leaned

forward and whispered, "The duke is advertising. For a wife!"

"A wife?" Penelope repeated, certain that she must have misheard.

"Yes, indeed," Mr. MacLeod said. "It seems the new duke finds himself in need of a bride in order to secure his inheritance. Rather than approaching a female of his acquaintance, he has apparently decided to advertise for one who will suit his requirements."

"Surely this is a jest," Penelope said.

"It is no jest. The *Gazette* sent a correspondent to speak with Mr. Forsythe, the duke's solicitor. He confirmed the terms of the will. The new duke must be married within the month," Roger Lawton said, as he and his wife, Anne, joined their circle.

Roger was of an age with her own brother, James, but whereas James seemed prematurely middle-aged, Roger was still youthful, with a mischievous sense of humor. Once their families had hoped that she and Roger would make a match, but in time they had come to realize that this was impossible. She valued Roger as a friend, but he could never take the place of her first love. No man could, which was why she had vowed to remain single.

And she was genuinely happy that Roger had found Anne, who clearly doted on her husband.

"I do not understand. Why should a nobleman, indeed, why should any man advertise to seek a wife? Surely that is madness," Anne Lawton observed.

"On the contrary, I find it a most logical course of action," Roger replied.

"Tell me you are jesting," Anne said.

"Of course I am, sweetheart," Roger said, taking one of his wife's hands in his. "I daresay the poor duke was overcome with despondency when he learned that you were wed, and no longer available. Fearing he could find no one to equal you, he resorted to this last desperate measure."

Anne Lawton blushed. "Now you are mocking me," she said, with pretend severity.

"The duke mocks us all," Mr. MacLeod intoned. "Such an advertisement reduces marriage to the level of mere commerce. But he is caught in his own trap. Only a woman whose greed outweighs her decency would respond to such an advertisement. I wish the duke the joy of his mercenary bride."

Penelope could not comprehend what manner of gentleman could have placed such an advertisement. He must be either an eccentric of the first water or a cynical misogynist. What could he hope to gain with this scheme? No decent woman would respond to such an impertinent offer.

Further musings were cut off when Mrs. Lawton summoned the party to dinner. Conversation was general, but soon turned back to the subject of the new duke and his strange behavior. His character was dissected at length, a process somewhat hampered by the fact that none of those present had ever met the new Duke of Torringford, who appeared to have lived a quiet country life before his recent elevation to the peerage. Nonetheless, many felt free to speculate on his character and motivations, based on the little they knew. Mr. MacLeod cast dark aspersions on the duke's character, while Mrs. Lawton charitably attributed his folly to senility brought on by his presumably advanced years.

Even Harriet Lawton, who normally disdained society gossip, was inspired to join the discussion. "For my part, I see nothing wrong with his advertisement," she said. "Indeed, such a logical approach to finding a mate speaks of a scientific bent of mind. Instead of condemning this gentleman we should be praising him, as a proponent of rationality in all things."

"Surely, Miss Lawton, you would never consider answering such an advertisement yourself," Mr. MacLeod intoned.

"I will have to consider the matter," Harriet Lawton said.

Horrified, Penelope glanced over at her friend, and was relieved to see the twinkle in her eyes that meant Harriet was jesting.

"You will do no such thing," Mrs. Lawton proclaimed. "And now, I think we should turn our attention to more worthy subjects. Mrs. Spenser, since you have recently returned from London, perhaps you would care to share with us your impressions?"

Following their hostess's lead, the conversation turned to less scandalous topics.

After dinner, the group proceeded by carriage to the University Lecture Hall, where the friends of the Royal Astronomical Society held their monthly gatherings.

Mr. Creighton was a gifted speaker, but for once his words failed to capture Penelope's attention. Instead her thoughts kept returning to this morning's unsettling conversation with her brother. If her brother were to marry Miss Carstairs, what would she do? Surely they could all rub along together in a civilized fashion, could they not?

Her distraction continued, as she joined the Lawtons in the carriage for the journey homeward.

She was startled out of her reverie as Harriet Lawton touched her arm.

"Will you join us?" Harriet Lawton asked.

She must have missed the question. "I am sorry, I was woolgathering," Penelope said. "What was your question?"

"There is to be a public subscription next month, to raise funds for the building of the new observatory. Will you help us pen the letters to the patrons?"

"Of course," Penelope said. Her small inheritance from her parents allowed her to donate only modest sums to such public projects, so instead she donated her time and enthusiasm.

"Something has been troubling you all evening," Harriet Lawton observed softly. "Do you care to share it?"

"The literary society will need to find another place to hold our gatherings. James has decided that he is no longer willing for me to play hostess," Penelope said.

"And does this have anything to do with a certain Miss Carstairs?"

"Miss Carstairs does not care for such gatherings, and James wishes to please her in all things."

Harriet reached over and grasped her gloved hand in hers, giving her a reassuring squeeze. "There is no need to worry. My mother will be glad to host the society."

"Roger and I would be glad to take part as well," Anne Lawton said from the opposite bench, as her husband nodded.

"That is most kind of you," Penelope said.

But in truth, the hosting of the literary meetings was the least of her worries. Rather, it was the change in her brother's attitude that concerned her. As an unmarried gentlewoman, she was dependent upon her brother's goodwill. Till now, he had been most indulgent of her foibles. But if he should change his attitude—

"Miss Carstairs seems a pleasant enough girl," Anne Lawton said, breaking into her gloomy thoughts. "If she and your brother do make a match, I am certain you will soon learn to enjoy each other's company."

"And if not, well then, I know Mr. Ian MacLeod would be honored to have you as his wife. I would be happy to have a word with him, to convince him to press his suit," Roger Lawton added.

Penelope laughed, as he had no doubt intended. "Matters are not nearly so grave, but I thank you for your kindness."

She pasted a smile on her face, and banished her worries from her mind. It was foolish to fret herself over possibilities that might never come to be. For all she knew, Miss Carstairs might disdain her brother's suit, and then Penelope would feel foolish indeed.

"Come now, enough of gloomy thoughts," she said. "Pray tell me, what thought you of tonight's lecture? Mr. Creighton's plan to map the comets once the new observatory is built sounds most ambitious. Do you think he will one day rival the fame of Sir Edmund Halley?"

THREE

Marcus Heywood entered his brother's chamber and slammed the door shut behind him.

"How could you let this happen?" he demanded.

Reginald wilted under his regard. "Marcus, you know I would never—"

"But you did. You penned that cursed missive, so this disaster is your making," Marcus interrupted. He had nursed the cold fury within him for the past two days, and he would not be gainsaid. "I could scarcely believe my eyes when I read the advertisement in the *Edinburgh Courant*. The next day I expected to read a retraction, but instead I find an entire column devoted to my private affairs. What were you thinking?"

He paced back and forth across the small bedchamber, unable to stay still.

Reginald rose to face his brother. He swallowed, and then began. "Yes, I penned that foolish advertisement. And the next morning, after you left, I was still in my cups when I gave the bootboy what I thought was the advertisement for the kennel master, and bade him bring it to the newspaper office without delay. If I had waited until I was sober enough to read what I had written, I could have avoided this whole mess. But what's done is done. I take full blame for what happened."

This much Marcus had been able to reason out for himself. He could still taste the bitter shock he had felt, when opening up the newspaper, he had turned to the commercial notices. Fully expecting to read the announcement that Marcus Heywood sought a new kennel master for the Greenfields estate, he had nearly choked on his coffee when he read the notice for a wife that Reginald had penned in jest.

"But why was there no explanation of the mistake? I expected to see an immediate retraction, and instead I find it treated with all seriousness, and news of my desperate search for a bride is carried in every paper," Marcus demanded.

Suddenly weary, he threw himself into a chair, stretching his long legs before him.

After a long look to judge his brother's temper, Reginald resumed his own seat.

"For that, there is blame to share. The advertisement was printed in the afternoon edition. I was engaged to dine with Mark Clemens and a few others of his acquaintance that evening, and we then went to the opera. It was early morning before I returned to my rooms, and I did not know what had happened till someone mentioned it the next evening. By then, it was in all the Edinburgh papers. A correspondent had spoken with Mr. Forsythe, who was all too willing to confirm the details of our late cousin's will. Once I learned what had happened, I went to James McGregor. He was able to convince the *Courant* to cease printing the advertisement, but they were unwilling to print a retraction. They claimed they were unable to do so without your written confirmation. If truth be told, I think they knew the lie for what it was, but were far more interested in selling papers than in reporting the truth."

It was well known that scandals sold newspapers, and what could be more scandalous than a peer of the realm advertising for a bride? It was small wonder that the rival newspapers had soon joined in spreading the scurrilous tale.

"I wrote to the newspapers denouncing this as a hoax, and sent the letters by express messenger," Marcus said.

"I have not seen them," Reginald responded. "Perhaps they will be printed in this evening's editions."

Or perhaps not. He would have to speak with James McGregor, and see what could be done. Could he sue the newspapers for libel? But doing so would reveal that his brother Reginald had penned the false missive, and that would make him seem even more the fool. It was an impossible tangle.

He rubbed his face with his hands, as his weariness finally caught up with him. He had ridden hard, making the journey from Greenfields to Edinburgh in a mere day and a half. And yet with each mile he had ridden, he had known he was already too late. The brush of scandal had tarred him and his family, and it would take a long time before this tale was forgotten.

"Surely the scandal will die down once there is news of your marriage to Miss Dunne," Reginald said.

"If only that were true, I would indeed be a fortunate man," Marcus observed. "However Alice Dunne has made other plans. You remember Samuel Makepeace, do you not? He has accepted a position in London, to preach the gospel of Wesley to the ungodly poor. Miss Dunne has agreed to accompany him, as his wife."

"Oh," Reginald said, at a loss for words.

"Indeed," Marcus replied.

He had been surprised to find that Alice Dunne had spent these years awaiting another. It had been a blow to his pride, if not his heart. Still he had managed to sincerely congratulate her upon her forthcoming marriage, even as he wondered how she could prefer the life of an impoverished missionary to that of a noblewoman.

It was a stroke of luck that he had learned of her impending marriage before he made a fool of himself by offering for her. He could only wonder what the Dunnes now thought of him. Surely they knew him well enough to know that he was the victim of a dreadful hoax.

"I confess I am at a loss as to how to proceed," Marcus said. Reginald was one of the few people that he trusted enough to confide in. "James McGregor was not in his offices when I called there, but his clerk promised to send him over here as soon as he returned. Until then . . ."

"Until then, you had best keep to our rooms, as I have for these past days," Reginald said. "The Porters have done a fine job in barring correspondents from the common room, but they were lurking outside the entrance and in the streets. It was a mercy you were not accosted when you came into the inn."

"I am fortunate that they did not recognize me," Marcus said. "No doubt that will change soon enough."

Any hopes that Mr. James McGregor would find a way out of this mess were dashed when his solicitor arrived later that afternoon. Friends since their days at school together, James wasted no time on pleasantries, but instead came swiftly to the point.

"I tell you, Marcus, I don't see how this affair could be made any worse," James McGregor said. He placed a bulging satchel on the scarred wooden table of the sitting room, and then took a seat opposite Marcus.

Mr. Porter came in, bearing a tray with three tankards of ale. As Reginald closed the door behind the innkeeper, James took a long drink of his ale.

Reginald picked up his own tankard, and retreated to a seat at the far end of the table. Marcus had asked him to join them, but Reginald was still wary, acting as if he were waiting for Marcus or James to remind him that he was the cause of this current predicament.

"Is there no way to free myself from this tangle?" Marcus asked. "If we could invalidate the will then there would be no need to worry about this marriage. I could simply go back to Greenfields, and wait for the scandal to die down."

The faint hope he had nourished for the past days died as James McGregor sadly shook his head. "Forsythe may be an ass, but he is no fool. The will has no obvious defect. Of course you could always find some grounds to challenge it on, but such a challenge could take years to work its way through the chancery courts. And until that day—"

"And until that distant date I would still be responsible for my late cousin's debts," Marcus said.

"Indeed. I took the liberty of reviewing the situation with two colleagues whom I trust, and their opinions match my own. Pursuing a challenge to the will would be a waste of time and money, and in the end, it is more than likely that the court would decide to uphold the original will."

Marcus took a sip of dark ale, the bitter taste providing a fine match to his dark thoughts.

"Which means I must be married before the fortnight is over."

James McGregor nodded. "A damn shame, but

I see no other course. Unless you care to give up the inheritance and refuse payment of your cousin's debts?"

For a brief moment he was tempted, but he pushed the unworthy thought aside. No matter what society thought of him at the moment, Marcus knew himself to be an honorable man. And he would continue to behave as such, regardless of the personal cost.

"No, I can not do that. I will have to find a bride who is willing to take me."

James McGregor blinked. "But your brother said you had a bride in mind?"

"I did. But she had her eye on another," Marcus said, his neutral tone giving no hint of the humiliation he felt. He had been well paid for his vanity, for all those years he had spent imagining that he had only to make his decision and his chosen bride would be his. Instead, not even his new fortune and title were enough to win her regard.

James McGregor tactfully looked away, refusing to catch his eye.

There was a long silence, as the three contemplated Marcus's problem.

"I don't suppose you have any suggestions?" Reginald asked.

"The newspaper reports have made things difficult," James McGregor said diplomatically.

"You mean to say it has made the matter impossible," Marcus countered. "My character has been blackened and my name made into a laughingstock. What woman of good character or sense would want to involve herself in such a scandal? If you had a daughter, would you want her to marry a gentleman with my reputation?"

"Marcus, I know you will make a fine husband, and if my own sister was of age, I would recommend you to her without hesitation."

Alas, Julia McGregor was still in the schoolroom, and would not be ready for marriage for some years yet.

"And if you did not know me so well?"

"Then, well then, I suppose, I would have doubts," James McGregor said.

It was an honest answer. Marcus respected his friend for his bluntness.

"So my position is impossible," Marcus declared.

"Not quite. There are, after all, hundreds of women who are willing to fill the position. I have letters from as far away as Wales, from young women eager to become the next Duchess of Torringford."

James McGregor unbuckled the straps on his satchel, and reaching in, withdrew two stacks of paper, one large and one small, each tied up with blue ribbon.

"Have you gone mad?" Marcus demanded.

"Who knows what kind of women replied to this advertisement?" Reginald asked. "Surely only a woman of dubious character and morals would even consider writing to a stranger in this fashion."

"That is what I thought as well," James McGregor said. "And indeed, most of the letters appear to be from women who meet none of the qualifications you listed. But there were a few I thought promising."

Marcus swallowed heavily. He could not be hearing this. This was not happening. It was all an insane dream, and at any moment he would wake up. "James, are you recommending that I choose my bride from among those lackwits who responded to that insane advertisement?"

"Do you have a better plan?"

Indeed he did not, which was why he was so angry. "I would do just as well to propose to the first woman I met on the street."

"Such a plan has its own risks. I realize this is strange, but I can see no alternative. At least you know the women who wrote are willing to take you on, despite the scandal."

"So how do we proceed? A lottery?" Reginald asked.

"No," James McGregor said, fixing Reginald with a stern look. "I have taken the liberty of selecting a half-dozen candidates who live within a day's journey of Edinburgh. If you agree, I will invite each of them for an interview."

"And if none of them suit?"

"Then you are no worse off than before," James McGregor countered.

It was sheer folly, and yet the idea had a certain appeal. After all he was not committing to marry any of these women. Just to meet them. How difficult could that be?

"And you think one of these would make a suitable bride?"

James McGregor withdrew the top letter and handed it to him. "See for yourself," he said.

"Miss Penelope Hastings," Marcus said, glancing at the elegantly penned missive. "A gentlewoman of one-and-twenty years. Modesty is not one of her virtues, although she does describe herself as skilled at household management, and as a patroness of the arts."

James McGregor nodded. "I will admit I was surprised to find her among those who responded. Miss Hastings is from a fine old Edinburgh family. She has an unsullied reputation, and is well thought of among the literary set."

"And yet she writes to offer herself in marriage to a stranger," Marcus said.

Such recklessness did not speak well of either her intelligence or her common sense. And this woman was one of the best candidates that McGregor had been able to find. He shuddered to think of those candidates who had not met McGregor's standards.

Still, what choice did he have?

"You win," he said. "I will meet this paragon Miss Hastings, and a half-dozen others you find unobjectionable. We will give this scheme of yours a chance."

And if this did not work, he could always make his way to the market square in Old Town, and offer himself for sale to the highest bidder. Such folly could hardly damage his reputation any further.

FOUR

The hackney carriage drew to a stop at the end of Jacob's Lane.

"I can take you nae farther," the coachman called down through the open trapdoor on the roof. "The way ahead is blocked."

Penelope Hastings glanced out the window, and saw that the road ahead was indeed blocked by an overturned cart. A small crowd, no doubt of idlers drawn to the spectacle, had spilled from the sidewalks into the street, and were adding their own share of confusion to the mix.

"Come now, Mary," she instructed her maid. "We are in luck that the day is fine, since we will have to walk the rest."

Descending from the carriage, she paid the driver, and then dismissed him. As she led the way, Mary clumping dutifully behind, she kept her eyes open for number 27. As she drew near, she realized that the building she sought was in the middle of the commotion.

With her parasol in hand, she forced her way

through the crowd of idlers, and mounted the stairs. A few of the men called impertinent suggestions up after her, but she paid no attention to their cries. Although she did wonder what Edinburgh was coming to, that such idlers could be found in a respectable neighborhood in the very middle of the day.

Inside, at least, all was quiet. A clerk greeted her respectfully, and after instructing Mary to wait for her, Penelope followed the clerk into a small sitting room.

In her mind she had imagined the solicitor would be a forbidding personage, withered and stooped with age, perhaps wearing a wig. Nothing could have been further from the truth, for Mr. McGregor proved to be an ordinary-looking man, with sandy blond hair and a kind face. He looked to be of an age with her brother James, which made him seem far too young for such a responsible position.

Mr. McGregor rose as she entered, and gave her a short bow.

"Miss Hastings, it was good of you to come, with such brief notice. Please, take a seat," he said.

She sat down in a straight-backed chair, and Mr. McGregor resumed his own seat.

He stared at her for a moment, as if scrutinizing her character, and she returned his gaze steadily. His face colored, as if in realization of his impertinence.

"Perhaps you can explain why you summoned

me?" she asked, when it seemed clear that he had no intention of breaking the silence.

"My client, the Duke of Torringford, wishes to speak with you, regarding the proposal that you sent."

Suddenly everything became clear. She had wondered why a solicitor would wish to speak to her, of all people, rather than to her brother, as head of the family. Now it all made sense.

"The duke has read our proposal? May I take it that he is interested?"

It was strange that the duke had chosen to contact her, rather than direct his inquiry to Mr. Creighton, or to the members of the society. But a duke must be allowed his own eccentricities, and if he wished to help underwrite the new observatory, who was she to quibble over his manner of conducting his affairs? She did not know the duke personally, but something about his name seemed familiar. After all, she had addressed hundreds of letters on behalf of the society. She could hardly be expected to remember every name.

"I believe I may say that there were elements of your letter that His Grace found intriguing, although naturally I can not claim to know his mind. Still, he wished to speak to you and to several other candidates before reaching any kind of decision," Mr. McGregor said.

So there was more than one organization vying for the duke's patronage. No doubt the duke had conditions of his own that would have to be met before he would agree to be a sponsor. Such was often the way with great noblemen, who required that their generosity be publicly acknowledged. Perhaps he wished for a building to be named in his honor, or a permanent seat on the board of directors.

"Naturally I would be happy to speak with His Grace, to assure him of the worthiness of this proposal," Penelope said, trying to express her sincere conviction. "But I am just one of several on the board of the society. I am certain Mr. Creighton, or indeed, Sir Archibald Cavendish, the head of our society, can best speak to the duke and answer any questions he may have about the project."

Mr. McGregor's eyes widened in surprise. "The project? You call this a project?"

"The full name is the Select Committee for the Establishment of a Royal Scottish Astronomical Observatory, but in truth it is simpler to refer to it as the project," she explained.

Mr. McGregor shook his head, as if in amazement. She wondered why a duke would employ a solicitor who had difficulty grasping such a simple concept. Perhaps if she explained things from the beginning.

"You did read the proposal from the committee, did you not?" she asked.

"I am afraid there has been some mistake. I did not ask you here to discuss the stargazing society. You were invited here to discuss the letter you sent to the duke. The letter in which you proposed yourself as a candidate for marriage."

Penelope swallowed hard. "Marriage?"

"Yes."

Suddenly she remembered precisely who the Duke of Torringford was, and why his name had sounded so familiar. She gulped again, as she realized the impossible muddle that she had landed in.

"I assure you, I penned no such note," she said tersely. She rose to her feet, preparing to end the interview.

There was a faint click, and then the sound of the door opening behind her.

"Your Grace, we have been expecting you," Mr. McGregor said, rising to his feet.

"No, we have not," Penelope said. She turned to face the newcomer.

She had her second surprise of the day. Based on the discussions at the dinner party, Penelope had assumed the new duke was a corpulent lecher, so elderly or repulsive that he could have no hope of winning a bride on his own merits. Nothing could have been further from the truth. The Duke of Torringford was a well-built man, perhaps in his late twenties, with dark brown hair and brown eyes. His plainly tailored blue jacket and tan pants revealed a powerful body, while his sun-browned complexion showed a man used to country life.

She wondered what Harriet Lawton would have thought, had the solicitor summoned her instead.

"Your Grace, may I present Miss Penelope Hastings?" Mr. McGregor said. "Miss Hastings, this is Marcus Heywood, the Duke of Torringford."

The duke crossed the few feet that separated them, and made a deep bow. "It is a pleasure to make your acquaintance," he said.

Penelope's anger grew as his eyes swept over her, as if measuring her on some internal scale. What right had these men to judge her, as if she were a brood mare on display?

"I can not share your sentiments," Penelope said. "I had just informed your solicitor that a mistake has been made. I have no interest in marriage, and even if I did, I would never lower myself to consider such an absurd scheme as yours."

The duke's eyes flashed with anger. "Then you deny writing a letter in response to the advertisement?"

"Of course," she said. What kind of fool did they take her for?

Mr. McGregor cleared his throat. "Perhaps you would like to reconsider your answer," he said.

She turned, and saw that he held out a piece of paper. Her eyes skimmed the sheet, pausing at the signature. That was indeed her name and direction signed at the bottom.

"I recognize the hand," she said slowly. The elegant swirls of old-fashioned copperplate had become familiar to her in these last months.

"Then you did write it," the duke said.

She shook her head. "I did not say that. I said I recognized the hand. I am afraid that I have been the victim of a cruel hoax."

She folded the letter carefully and then slipped it into her reticule.

The duke's eyes searched her face, and then he smiled in rueful sympathy. "Pray accept my sympathies. I know all too well what it is to be the victim of a jest," he said.

"Thank you. And now, I think it best if I take my leave."

"Perhaps one day we may meet again, in more pleasant circumstances."

"We can hardly meet in worse," she said.

This won her another smile, and the duke held the door for her as she left.

She returned to the foyer, where she found her maid busy gossiping with the clerks. Catching sight of her mistress, Mary hastily cut her conversation short, and came over to help Penelope don her cloak.

"Shall I have one of my clerks summon a hackney?" Mary asked.

"No, I think we will walk for a bit," Penelope said. "I would like to stop at Hedges' to see if the new novels have arrived."

And the walk would give her time to gather her thoughts. Should she tell her brother what had happened? Even if she showed him the letter, would he believe her? Or would he find some way to blame this on her? There was no denying that the letter was a malicious act. But if she confronted Miss Carstairs, the scheming minx was sure to deny everything. And she had a sinking feeling that if she forced her brother to choose between them, his infatuation would lead him to believe Miss Carstairs over his own sister.

* * *

In the end, Penelope decided she would say nothing of the hoax to her brother. It would serve no purpose, save to drive a wedge between them. However, the next time she saw her brother's intended, she would let Miss Carstairs know that her deceit had been discovered. It was possible that the letter had been written in a momentary fit of pique. Surely Miss Carstairs must regret her rash action, and once she realized that Penelope had discovered her plan, perhaps that would be enough to dissuade her from attempting any other such tricks.

For her own part, Penelope resolved to treat Miss Carstairs with all civility. She would give the young woman no chance to complain of her treatment at Penelope's hands.

Her good resolution turned out for naught, for two days after her encounter with the duke she returned from an afternoon lecture to find her brother pacing the hall. His cravat was half undone, and his face was flushed.

"James, is something wrong?" Penelope asked, as she handed her cloak to the footman.

James shot her a venomous glare. "How can you ask that? Did you think I would not hear of your scandalous behavior? How much longer were you planning on waiting before you told me?"

His angry tirade confused her. "I do not know what has you in an uproar. I am certain it must be a simple misunderstanding."

"Misunderstanding?" His voice cracked. "It is a nightmare!"

From the corner of her eye she saw the footman Robin, still clutching the coat, hanging on every word.

"This is hardly the place for such a discussion," she said. "Come now, and we will talk in private."

She led the way to her sitting room, and after a moment heard James's footsteps behind her. He slammed the door behind them.

"It is a little late for discretion, since news of your escapade is in all the papers. If the servants haven't heard of it by now, they will have by this evening."

A sudden horrible suspicion crossed her mind. "Just what is it that you think I have done?"

It couldn't be, she told herself. And yet his next words proved her worst fears had come true.

"When I went to the club today, I found myself the subject of sly congratulations. Imagine my surprise when I learned that my sister was to become a duchess."

"James, I can explain—" she began.

"No," he said, raising his right hand to cut off her words. "The gossip pages reported this morning that a certain Miss Penelope H—of Edinburgh had taken her love of rationalism to a new height by applying for the position of Duchess of Torringford. The notorious duke, after meeting the woman in question, was pleased to accept her proposal."

"Good heavens." She sank down on the sofa. This was worse than she had imagined. "But how could this have happened?"

"You were recognized leaving the solicitor's office." James leaned up against the mantel, resting one arm against it. "Did you even once think of how this would look? What this would do to our family's reputation?"

"I am not to blame," Penelope said. "I did not write to the duke."

"But you did meet with him, did you not?"

"Yes, but it was a mistake. He had received a letter with my name on it."

"And you expect me to believe this tale? Why would someone forge a letter with your name? Why would you agree to meet with the duke, if not to discuss his absurd search for a wife?"

"I thought he wished to become a patron of the Astronomical Society. Once I realized my mistake, I took my leave," Penelope said. "As for the letter, you will have to ask Miss Carstairs why she penned the missive and signed my name."

Her brother's eyes narrowed. "Is it not enough that you blacken our name? Now you must drag an innocent into this as well?"

"I can show you the letter. You will have to agree it is not my hand," Penelope said.

James shook his head. "No doubt you had one of your bluestocking friends write it out, in an attempt to shift blame."

"How can you believe me capable of such deceit?"

"How can I not?" he retorted. "If all was innocent, why did you not tell me at once? Why not the day you met the duke? Why must I find this out through scurrilous gossip?"

She wished fiercely that she could turn back the hands of the clock. If only she hadn't agreed to meet the solicitor. If she had only known that the Duke of Torringford was Mr. McGregor's client. If she had only spoken to her brother that day.

If only. But there was no changing the past. Now they must face the future.

"I met the duke, as I told you, and I explained the mistake. We parted cordially, but there was no mention of marriage. The newspaper reports are wrong. The scandal is unfortunate, but in a few weeks, after the duke has chosen his bride, this episode will be forgotten."

"No," James said. "If you lived a blameless life for the next hundred years, you would still not be able to live down the scandal. Bad enough that society thinks you proposed to the duke. How will it look when he refuses your offer and marries another?"

She hadn't thought of that.

James kept on speaking. "You have two choices. You will marry this duke, and the two of you can attempt to restore your tarnished honor. Or, if you choose to remain single, you will retire to the cottage Great Aunt Ivers left you in Selvay Firth."

"Selvay Firth? You can not be serious." Selvay Firth was a small coastal village a hundred miles north of Edinburgh. It was a mere pinprick on the map, a speck too insignificant for anything of note to have happened there. Penelope had been there once, when her mother had taken her to visit her ailing aunt. She had no wish to return.

"And if I refuse?" she asked.

"You have no choice," James said, pushing himself away from the mantel and drawing himself up stiffly. "Until your marriage, I control your inheritance. I will not allow you to remain in Edinburgh, a living reminder of the disgrace you have brought upon us. Marriage or banishment to the country. It is your decision."

She looked in his face for some sign of kindness or affection, but there was only scorn in his eyes and the tight set of his mouth. With the mask of civility stripped away, she knew at this moment that her brother hated her, although she was at a loss to explain why.

Her own anger rose hot and sudden. "I thank you for the benefit of your wisdom, dear brother," she said. "I will take a few days to consider my position."

"A week, no longer," he said.

"A week it is," she answered. "And lest I forget, I will take this moment now to wish you and Miss Carstairs joy. I see now that you are perfectly suited for one another."

With that she rose, and swept from the room.

Once out of sight of her brother, she found it hard to maintain her composure. To think that only a few days ago she had been fretting over the possibility of having to live in a house presided over by Amelia Carstairs. Now she could not even hope for that dubious pleasure.

As an unmarried woman, her choices were few indeed. Even if she somehow persuaded James to release her inheritance, she could not set up her own household and expect society to accept her. Not after this scandal. A respectable young woman of one-and-twenty simply did not live on her own, with no female relatives to countenance her. It was unheard of.

And even if they were willing to take her in, she could not inflict her presence on the Lawtons. Leaving her brother's household would be taken as a sign of guilt, and the taint on Penelope's good name would inevitably tarnish Harriet's reputation and that of her sisters.

She could give in to her brother, and accept banishment to Selvay Firth. But she could not imagine leaving Edinburgh. It was the center of her world. Everything was here. Her friends, her societies, her causes, every activity that filled her days and nights was within the city walls. Exile to a remote village was a cruel punishment indeed.

Or she could marry. And there was only one candidate, the Duke of Torringford. No other gentleman would want a wife with Penelope's reputation. Even Mr. Ian MacLeod had no doubt forsworn his infatuation for her, in light of this scandal.

She faced a difficult choice indeed, and she wondered whom of her friends she could trust to advise her.

FIVE

"His Grace, the Duke of Torringford," the footman intoned.

Marcus's stomach clenched with nervous anticipation as he entered the small sitting room.

"Miss Hastings, I appreciate your agreeing to see me," he said.

"Your letter was most insistent, Your Grace." Her gaze drifted to the footman behind him. "That will be all, Robin. And kindly shut the door," she said firmly.

He sat on the edge of a chair, hoping he did not look as uneasy as he felt inside. He had not felt this nervous in years. But then again, it was not every day you called upon a virtual stranger and attempted to convince her to become your wife.

Especially when the lady in question had already made it quite clear that she had no interest in marrying him. It was an ironic twist of fate. Out of the seven candidates James McGregor had presented for his inspection, there had been only one with whom he felt any sort of connection. And she was there only because of a mistake.

Perhaps his attraction was because of that very mistake. Perhaps it was the fact that unlike the others, Miss Hastings had not been trying to curry his favor. Instead she had been dignified, and honest to the point of bluntness. That was a trait that he could admire.

And her appearance was pleasing as well. Her dark auburn hair curled softly around her face, bringing attention to her inquisitive hazel eyes. And the green of her dress, the green of the newly sprouted corn, emphasized her creamy complexion.

All things considered, he could do far worse for himself. Much worse. Now if only he could convince her the marriage would be in her best interests as well.

"Your Grace?" Miss Hastings prompted.

He flushed, realizing that he had been lost in his own thoughts.

"Please, call me Marcus. Being called Your Grace makes me feel as if I am an ancient, and surely there is no need for formality," he said with a smile.

"Your Grace," she said, pointedly rejecting his overture. "I thought we had said all that we had to say to one another."

"I came to make my apologies to you, and to your family," he said.

"Apologies?"

"Surely you have seen the newspaper reports."

"Indeed we have. But unless you were the one who gave my name to the correspondents, I do not see that you have anything to apologize for," Miss Hastings said.

"It was not me. I do not know how they learned of our meeting," he said. James McGregor suspected one of his clerks had been gossiping with the newspaper correspondents. But there was no proof, and so he would keep his suspicions to himself. "Nonetheless, the situation is of my making, and I bear the blame for dragging you into this."

"The blame is not wholly yours. A portion must be laid at the door of the newspapers, who are so quick to report scandal without pausing to verify the truth. Not to mention that we would never have met, had not a false friend decided to send in my name as a jest."

He had come here expecting anger and condemnation, but her reasoned civility surprised him.

"You are generous, but still it falls upon me to make amends. I realize your reputation has been damaged, and I can offer no amends other than to suggest that we be married."

"No," she said, rising to her feet. "If that is what you came to say, then this conversation is over."

"Wait," he said, reaching out to clasp her hand. "Hear me out."

She looked at him, and then nodded. He released her hand, and she took her seat.

He felt a faint shimmer of hope. If she was truly set against the match, his light touch would not have stopped her from leaving. So at least a part of her was willing to listen to his proposal.

"By now the entire kingdom knows that I must marry within the week, in order to fulfill the conditions of the late duke's will."

"And is securing that fortune so important that you made a fool out of yourself with that ridiculous advertisement?" she asked.

"No, the advertisement was a mistake. A poor jest, scribbled in drunken folly, and sent to the newspaper by accident. By the time I learned of it, the newspapers had decided on their own version of the truth and would not listen to reason."

"So why continue the charade? Why seek to interview those women who had responded?"

How could he explain without making himself sound more of a fool than he was?

"Once the story was out, it seemed I had no other choice. The scandal caused all other doors to be barred to me." He shrugged helplessly. "I let McGregor pick the best of the lot. He knew of your family, so the letter with your name on it was among them."

"And would you really marry a stranger? Is the wealth that important to you?"

"Of course not. For my sake I would refuse the inheritance. I never wanted great wealth or a title. I would give it all back if I could. But I can't." He hesitated, then realized that only complete honesty would serve. "It seems I also inherited substantial debts, from my cousin George Wallace who had been in line for the dukedom. Over a hundred thousand pounds, at last reckoning."

"A hundred thousand pounds? Surely you are mistaken." Her hazel eyes widened in shock, just as his had when he first learned the news.

"A hundred thousand pounds," he repeated. "A monstrous sum to be certain, but only a small fraction of the duke's estate. So you see I have two choices, neither of them good. I can refuse the inheritance and go bankrupt trying to pay a fraction of my cousin's debts. Or I can give in to Torringford's whim and marry."

"And you have decided I will do as well as any other?" she asked. "Surely there is some woman of your acquaintance you could ask."

"There was, but she had found someone who suited her better. And I have no time in which to court another," he explained. "I promise you, this folly notwithstanding, I am considered to be of good character, an honorable landowner who cares for his family and tenants. My friends can attest to my virtues."

"But they will not offer their sisters or daughters in marriage," Penelope pointed out.

"What was I to do? Write to each of my acquaintances, telling them that I was desperately seeking a wife?"

Given time, he was certain he could have found a suitable bride among the women of his acquaintance. But that was the problem. There had been no time. And he had been so certain that Alice Dunne would accept him, more fool he.

"Is there another gentleman you planned to marry?" he asked, remembering his awkward meeting with Alice Dunne.

"No, I had no plans of marriage. Ever," Miss Hastings replied.

Such was unusual, in a woman of her age and class. She might be in mourning for some lost love, and had dedicated herself to spinsterhood in his memory. Perhaps she was one of the free thinkers, like Mary Shelley, who held that marriage represented a fatal compromise for a woman. Perhaps her parents' marriage had been infelicitous and had set her against the institution.

Or mayhaps there was another reason for her reluctance. Perhaps she was being kind, not stating the obvious. That she had no wish to marry him.

"In that case, I offer myself. A marriage of convenience, for both of us. I, to secure my inheritance, and you to reclaim your good name."

"Do you really think marriage will restore my reputation?"

"All things are possible, in time. Especially since as the Duchess of Torringford, you will be in a position to lead society. And to be a true patroness of the arts and sciences, if you so wish."

He could see her turning the idea over in her mind. He held his breath, hoping her answer would be yes.

"Then I agree," she said. "It seems my choices

are marriage, or a dilapidated cottage in Selvay Firth."

Relief flooded through him, and he released the breath he had been holding. He realized that he had been unconsciously expecting her to reject him.

"A cottage?" he asked, as he gathered his thoughts.

"My brother's suggestion," Miss Hastings replied.

"I am pleased to find that you hold me in higher esteem than a mere cottage," he said.

"It was a difficult choice, to be certain." She smiled, inviting him to share in the jest.

It was amazing how a simple smile could transform her appearance, and he realized for the first time that his intended was indeed out of the ordinary. He wondered what it would have been like had they met under ordinary circumstances. Would he have even noticed her? Would she have noticed him?

He knew himself for a lucky man. His intended was pretty, intelligent, and had a dry sense of humor. It was possible that they could indeed make a success out of their marriage. For the first time in a fortnight he felt hopeful about his future.

Now that he had secured her permission, he saw no need to delay. Better that they be married in haste, before Penelope had a chance to change her mind.

"A civil ceremony is required. I will ask McGre-

gor to make the arrangements. Is Saturday accept-
able to you?"

She swallowed nervously, but maintained her
composure. Saturday was just three days away.
"Saturday will be agreeable."

"Until then," he said, rising and taking her
hand. He bowed over it.

Her slim hand tightened its grip on his. "Until
Saturday," she replied.

"The sash is crooked, I can feel it," Penelope
declared, twisting herself around as she tried to
see the back of her gown.

"The sash is fine," Harriet Lawton said, coming
to stand beside her friend. "The gown is perfect.
You look beautiful."

Penelope frowned doubtfully, wishing there was
a mirror so she could check her own reflection.
But the small antechamber held nothing except a
small table and a half-dozen chairs.

"I should have worn the yellow silk that I had
made for Easter," she said.

She had hesitated up until the last possible instant, before deciding upon the pale blue gown
with lace trim that she now wore.

"Sit," Harriet urged her, "you are fretting over
nothing, and you will wear a hole in the carpet
with your pacing."

Harriet took a seat, and after a moment Penelope followed her friend's example.

"I know you well enough to know it is not the

gown that has made you so nervous. If you have doubts about this arrangement, then now is the time to speak. There is still time to call this mad scheme off," Harriet said.

Trust Harriet to see through her. Indeed, Penelope was nervous, more nervous than she had ever been before. A part of her felt that this was a bizarre dream, and that at any moment she would wake up and laugh at her fanciful imagination. But the rest of her knew that this was all too real. In a mere quarter hour's time, she would be Penelope Hastings no longer. She would be the Duchess of Torringford, having pledged herself to a gentleman who was still very much a stranger.

"I suppose I am nervous," she confessed. "But are not all brides nervous on their wedding day?"

"Yes, but generally they are at least acquainted with their prospective husbands. You know practically nothing about this man you are to marry. For all you know, he could be a rake and a lecher."

"He is nothing of the sort," Penelope said. "It is true that we have only spoken briefly, but I feel he is a kind man, a gentleman who will behave with honor."

"Honor," Harriet echoed. "Is that all you wish for from your marriage? What about those things we used to talk of? True love? A joyous union of souls?"

Penelope shrugged, trying to pretend that she was unconcerned. What matter that this was hardly the type of union that inspired the poets? Hundreds of women across England married for convenience, and they were no worse off than many who married for love. And it was not as if she had chosen this of her own free will.

"This is a business arrangement, not a love match. As long as both parties enter into the marriage with open eyes and a spirit of accommodation, I see no reason why we should not make a success of this marriage. Indeed, we will likely fare better than many who marry in impetuous haste, only to later regret their decisions," Penelope said.

"As your friend, I must say that I do not like this. If you were to be married, it should be to someone you love with your whole heart. Someone like Stephen Wolcott."

Penelope winced. Even after five years, it still hurt to hear his name. "Perhaps there was a time when I dreamed of a different kind of marriage. But I am older and wiser now. And having given my heart once, it is not in my nature to fall in love again."

She smiled ruefully. "Now that sounded like I was asking for pity, but I am not, I assure you. You must wish me happiness instead. This will all turn out for the best, you will see," she said, reassuring herself at the same time as she reassured her friend.

"I wish you all the happiness you so justly deserve," Harriet said.

There was a soft rap at the door, and then it opened to reveal Mr. McGregor. "His Grace has arrived. If you ladies are ready?"

"Of course," Penelope said. There was no point in delay. She was as ready as she would ever be.

She followed Mr. McGregor into his office, where the duke was waiting, and was introduced to his brother Reginald Heywood, who would act as one of the two witnesses, with Harriet serving as the second. Under Scottish law, a couple could be married simply by stating the fact of their marriage in front of two witnesses.

James, for all his insistence on this marriage, had refused to accompany her. She was grateful that no one thought to question his absence.

Prompted by the solicitor, she stated her intention to be wed in a clear firm voice, and was echoed by the duke. Then they each signed the documents that Mr. McGregor had drawn up, and the witnesses affixed their own signatures.

In less than five minutes it was over. Her life had changed irrevocably.

"Your Graces, may I be the first to congratulate you," Mr. McGregor said. "I wish you every happiness."

Penelope and Marcus thanked him for his sentiments, and then Reginald Hastings and Harriet Lawton added their own wishes for the couple's future happiness. The exchange of compliments took far longer than the wedding vows.

Everyone was doing their best to appear as if there were nothing out of the ordinary in this marriage. It was all so civilized and polite. A part of Penelope appreciated their courtesy. And another part wanted to scream in frustration, and tell the others that there was no need for such pretense.

She glanced over at the duke, who wore a mask of grave courtesy. She wondered what he was thinking. Did he harbor regrets of his own? She knew how far this wedding was from her own imaginings as a young woman. Had he, too, imagined a different future for himself? A love match, perhaps, or a marriage of affection and mutual regard?

Enough, she thought to herself. Such musings had no place. What was done was done, and now she and her new husband would learn to make the best of their future.

"If you are ready, I think we should take our leave," the duke said. "We have a long journey ahead of us."

"Indeed," Penelope agreed, meaning not just the wedding trip stretching out before them. It was the rest of their lives.

SIX

For their wedding trip, Marcus had proposed traveling to the duke's family seat, which was located in the Lake District. It was fitting that the duke and his new bride inspect the ancestral properties that he had inherited. And their absence from Scotland would give a chance for the gossip regarding their marriage to die down. Hopefully, by the time they returned, society would have found other unfortunates to make the target of their speculations.

Penelope had agreed to the plan, seeing the wisdom of absenting herself from Edinburgh. She needed time to adjust to her new status. And the journey would give her a chance to get to know this man who was now her husband.

The carriage swayed gently as they left the city of Edinburgh. It was a strange feeling, leaving the city where she had spent her whole life. Except for the childhood journey to Selvay Firth, she had never left. And now she was to journey to England.

After politely inquiring as to her comfort, the

duke fell silent. Unlike the gentlemen of her acquaintance, it appeared he was not a man much
given to conversation. Especially not with a woman
he barely knew, for all that she was his wife.

"I am looking forward to this journey,"
Penelope observed, compelled to break the awkward silence. "I have never visited England before,
and they say the Lake District is quite beautiful."

"The countryside is no match for our own, but
it is quite pleasant in its own way," the duke acknowledged.

"Can you tell me of the Torringford estate? How
long has it been the family seat? Is it landscaped
in the classical style or the romantic style?"

The duke shrugged his shoulders. "I do not
know. I have never had occasion to visit Torringford, before now."

"I see," Penelope said, although she did not
understand at all. Surely the late duke would have
wanted to become acquainted with his heir. And
it was only fitting that the heir familiarize himself
with his future responsibilities.

"My grandfather was the late duke's brother,"
Marcus explained. "With six sons of his own, the
duke had little reason to expect his title to fall to
our branch of the family. And since he and my
grandfather were estranged, our families had little
to do with one another."

Such estrangement did much to explain her
husband's obvious discomfort with his new station
in life, not to mention the oddity of the terms of
the old duke's will.

"And Reginald is your only brother, Your Grace?"

"Marcus," he corrected her. "I see no point in standing on ceremony."

"And Reginald is your only brother, Marcus?" she repeated, and was rewarded with one of his rare smiles.

"Yes. My mother died when we were both children, and my father died in a riding accident three years ago."

There was a flash of pain in his eyes before his face resumed its habitual tranquil mask. She felt a sudden surge of sympathy. "My parents died three years ago, as well," she said. "They fell victim to the fevers, which were particularly virulent that spring."

The fevers had swept through the city, claiming rich and poor alike. It had been brutally swift. First her father had fallen ill, and then her mother. They had died within days of each other, while neither she nor James suffered so much as the sniffles.

"I am sorry for your loss," he said, reaching to take her hand in his. The warmth of his hand on hers was a novel feeling.

"And you have a brother yourself, do you not?" he asked.

"Yes. James is the elder," she said.

"He did not join you today," Marcus observed.

It was her brother's hypocrisy that she found hardest to forgive. It was James who had insisted that marriage would restore her reputation, and yet having gotten his way, he did not have the courtesy to attend his only sister's wedding. No doubt the gossips would have a field day when they learned that tidbit.

He had not even met the man who was to be her husband. All the hasty arrangements had been made between their mutual solicitors.

"No, he did not. I daresay it will be some time before he sees fit to forgive what he sees as my scandalous conduct. Until he sees some benefit to be gained in the connection, we have little to fear that he will trouble us," she said bitterly.

"I can not understand such behavior, but he is not mine to judge," Marcus said. "You are your own mistress now. If you wish to have nothing to do with him, simply say so, and I will make certain he troubles you not."

It was kind of him to defend her, but she hastened to assure him that there was no need. "Even when civility is restored, I suspect we will have little enough to do with one another. Edinburgh society is diverse, and since James and I have quite different interests our circles rarely overlap."

The duke shook his head doubtfully. "And you have lived your whole life in Edinburgh?"

"Yes."

"Do you not find it tedious? For my own part, after a fortnight in Edinburgh, I am all too eager to return to the country."

"But Edinburgh is the jewel of Scotland, the Athens of the North," she exclaimed. "It is the center of arts, literature, and the sciences. Why only last week I was able to hear a reading of *nouvelle* poetry, an astronomy lecture, and attended an exhibition of paintings in the romantic style. Surely no other city, save perhaps London, offers one such intellectual society."

"Such things are not to everyone's taste," Marcus pointed out. "For my part, I would forego all those pleasures in exchange for an afternoon of hunting with my dogs."

"You ride to the hounds?"

"No, I raise beagles. North country hounds, actually. The finest gun dogs in all of Scotland," he said. His gaze grew unfocused and his face wore an expression of concern. "I hope Reginald makes a quick journey home. With no kennel master at present, I do not like leaving them alone so long. The kennel boys can only do so much."

"How many dogs do you have?" she asked.

"It varies depending on the time of year. The puppies this spring brought their numbers up to nearly a hundred."

"One hundred? You have one hundred dogs?" She could not imagine such a thing. How on earth did he tell them apart?

"Yes, but that is only for now. At the end of the summer, once the new puppies are trained, I will sell most of them off, saving the pick of the crop for next year's breeding."

"And do you have any trouble finding buyers?" How many hunting enthusiasts could there be in Scotland?

The look he gave her was one of pity for her

ignorance. "The dogs I breed are champions. If I could raise twice their number, I still could not satisfy all those who request them."

"Then why don't you raise twice as many?"

"With more dogs, I could not oversee their training myself. As it is, with McDougall gone, we will be hard-pressed to ensure they all receive proper training. Still, if the new kennel master is a man of worth, we should muddle through. But I will not rest easy until I am back at Greenfields and able to judge their progress for myself."

He fell silent. The animation that had lit his face as he talked about his beloved dogs slipped away, no doubt as he contemplated how many weeks it would be before he was able to return to his home.

Penelope was silent as well, lost in her musings as she contemplated the gulf that stretched between her and her new husband. This was not simply a matter of allowing their acquaintance to grow over time. The differences between them were profound. They had no points of common interests or experiences that would draw them together. Indeed, if she had tried, she could not have chosen a gentleman who was further from her own interests and sensibilities. It was fortunate that her affections were not engaged.

Penelope awoke to find that she had fallen asleep against the side of the carriage, and that

Marcus was shaking her gently. "We are stopping here for the night," he said.

She nodded, blinking the sleep from her eyes. The past few nights had not been restful, so it was no wonder she had fallen asleep.

Marcus descended from the carriage, and then held his hand to help her alight.

They stood in a muddy courtyard next to a gray stone building whose intricately carved sign proclaimed this to be Dunbarton's Inn and Coaching House. Glancing at the sky, she realized the sun was still some hours from setting.

"The roads were in fine shape and we made better time than I had expected," Marcus said, correctly interpreting her glance. "And I think we would both appreciate the opportunity for an early night."

She felt her cheeks begin to redden, and was grateful that a servant appeared to command Marcus's attention. An early night, indeed. Her wedding night, to be precise. Her lingering fatigue gave way to nervousness, and a queasy feeling in her stomach.

Logic told her that she had nothing to fear. All brides were inexperienced when it came to their wedding nights, and yet none suffered any lasting harm. The marriage act was a part of the natural order. Indeed, if the poets were to believed, there was much pleasure that could be found in such physical union, as the joining of two bodies echoed the joining of their souls.

Such rationalizations proved poor comfort,

when faced with the reality that in a few hours she would be expected to share a bed with this gentleman. They could scarcely agree upon a topic of conversation, and yet somehow they were expected to perform an act of unspeakable intimacy.

It was all a part of marriage, she reminded herself, as she followed Marcus's broad-shouldered figure into the coaching house.

The master of the inn met them, beaming with pride as he welcomed Their Graces to his humble establishment. His portly wife gave an awkward curtsy, and then offered to show them to their rooms.

They followed her up the stairs and down a short corridor. She threw open the door to the second to last room on the right-hand side. "Here is your bedchamber, Your Grace," she informed Penelope. "Your luggage will be up directly, and I have sent the maid to fetch hot water for washing."

Penelope glanced into the room, her eyes immediately drawn to the large canopied bed.

"And your chamber is adjacent, as you requested," the woman said to Marcus, opening a second door to reveal an even larger room with its own sitting area.

"We will dine in here at eight, if that is agreeable to my wife," Marcus said.

"That will be most agreeable," Penelope said, still puzzling out the meaning of the separate bedchambers. Perhaps it was simply a matter of convenience, ensuring that they would not be underfoot while dressing. And she could hardly raise the topic in front of the innkeeper's wife, nor the servants who even now carried in the trunks and began to arrange them.

"You will have a meal fit for your duchess, at eight," the innkeeper's wife promised.

"Thank you, that will be all," Marcus said, dismissing her.

Penelope entered her chamber, and Marcus entered his own, closing the door behind him.

The maid arrived a few minutes later, bearing hot water and clean towels, and followed by a servant carrying her trunk. The maid offered to assist her, but Penelope refused. She was accustomed to doing for herself. And she was grateful for the time alone, the chance to collect her thoughts. It had already been a momentous day, and there was still one more hurdle to be faced.

Precisely at eight, Penelope joined Marcus in his chamber for dinner. In honor of her ducal guests the cook had produced five lavish courses, but her efforts were for naught. To Penelope, each dish might as well have been sawdust, for all she could taste. Instead, as each course was cleared away, Penelope grew more and more nervous, anticipating what would occur once they were alone.

The burgundy wine was surprisingly fine, but she resisted the temptation to overindulge. It would serve neither of them if she became tipsy.

Her distraction was obvious, for Marcus noticed

it and inquired as to its cause. She told him it was simple fatigue from the journey, and he seemed to accept that explanation.

And then, before she knew it, the last of the plates was cleared away, and they were left alone with each other. Her heart began to pound and her palms to sweat.

Marcus rose from his seat, and crossed to her side of the table, pulling out her chair so she could rise as well. She glanced at his face, and then swiftly looked away. His expression was impossible to read, but she was afraid her own emotions showed all too plainly.

He took her right hand in his, and gave it a gentle squeeze. A reassuring touch. And then he leaned forward. She closed her eyes, and felt his lips brush her cheek.

"I thank you for your company," he said. "And now, it has been a long day, and so I bid you good night and a pleasant rest."

He released her hand, and his gaze moved toward her room.

It took a moment for his words to sink in. He had bid her good night. There was no reason for him to do so, if he had planned on joining her.

"And a good night to you as well," she said, scarcely able to contain her astonishment.

As she crossed into her own bedchamber, she heard the sound of the connecting door being firmly closed.

"Good night, indeed," she muttered, unaccountably furious.

Clearly he did not intend to consummate their marriage tonight. Perhaps it was because they were both fatigued from traveling. Perhaps he was simply being a gentleman, giving her a chance to get to know him before he claimed his rights.

Or a more lowering thought occurred to her. Maybe Marcus had no interest in making love with her. This was a marriage of convenience, after all. There was no passion between them, and there was no great hurry to produce an heir.

After all her earlier fears she knew she should be grateful for his forbearance, whatever his reasons. Instead she was angry. Surely he could have told her his intention beforehand, rather than leaving her to needlessly worry and fret. She might have been able to enjoy her dinner, if she had known that this was not to be her wedding night. But instead, in his high-handed way, he had made his decision, and taken it for granted that she would be pleased.

She might have been pleased, if she knew Marcus's mind. But instead she was left to guess his intentions. She had no idea if this was a single night's reprieve or a pattern that would exist for the length of their marriage. It was no wonder she was angry, she thought as she donned her nightgown and slipped into her chaste bed.

Not even to herself did she acknowledge that mixed in with her anger was a thread of disappointment. Instead she focused on her grievances.

This was hardly an auspicious start. Was this how Marcus envisioned their marriage? His role to decide and hers to comply with his wishes? In the days before the marriage, he had treated her as a rational creature, one who would be an equal partner in this match. Each had much to gain from the marriage, and a civil partnership would benefit them both. Or so he had allowed her to believe.

But now that they were wed, he was reverting to his true colors. Perhaps Selvay Firth was not as poor a choice as she had first thought. In choosing Marcus Heywood, she may have chosen a far more bitter form of punishment.

SEVEN

The first day's journey had passed without incident. Indeed, Marcus had found Penelope to be an agreeable traveling companion, not one of those silly women who felt the need to fill every moment with idle chatter. When she had fallen asleep, he had watched her thoughtfully, surprised by the surge of tenderness that he felt. She was his, he realized. His responsibility. His to care for.

The next day's journey was not nearly so pleasant. Even as they broke their fast, he could tell that his new bride was not pleased. Charitably, he attributed her mood to the earliness of the hour.

But as the day passed, her ill temper persisted. Not that she was openly petulant, or angry. She did not even complain. But her silence was icy, and the easiness that had existed between them on that first day was gone.

It did not take a scientist to realize that she was vexed with him. But when asked, she denied any such sentiment. She turned each inquiry away with polite dismissal. She was fine, she kept repeating, until he grew to hate the word.

It would take five days to reach Torringford Abbey, traveling by easy stages. He had deliberately planned the slow journey, out of consideration for his new bride. Now he found himself wishing that it was over. Anything would be better than this awkwardness.

It was impossible for two people to ignore each other while traveling in the confines of a coach, no matter how elegant or well sprung the vehicle. And yet she contrived to do just that. Yesterday Penelope had spent most of the day seemingly absorbed in a novel, or pretending to sleep. When they reached the inn, she had complained of fatigue, and used the excuse to dine alone.

Today, she had a new distraction, a guidebook that she had managed to acquire from somewhere.

"I trust you slept well?" Marcus asked.

Penelope made a noncommittal noise.

"It looks like it may rain today," he said.

There was no response. From his seat he had a very good view of the top of her bonnet, but he could see nothing of her expression. He was not used to being so thoroughly ignored. He wondered how she would react if he simply snatched the book from her hands and demanded that she look at him.

He waited a few moments, and tried again.

"I can not help notice that you seem . . . distracted," he said, for lack of a better word. "Is there something amiss? Something we should discuss?"

"Did you know the present Abbey is the third structure on that site?" Penelope asked.

"No, I know little of its history," he said. In fact he had never visited Torringford Abbey. Over the years there had been only a handful of occasions when the duke had felt the need to offer his hospitality to his country cousins. And the old feud had ensured that Marcus's father had refused all such invitations, scorning the branch of the family that had cast out his own father.

"According to the guidebook, when Elizabeth awarded the estate to the Earl of Knox, he tore down the original abbey and erected a mansion designed in the shape of the letter E in her honor. Apparently your ancestor was quite a favorite at court, and Elizabeth is known to have visited the new mansion on at least two occasions."

Marcus cared little for gossip, and even less for gossip about someone who had been dead for centuries.

"In seventeen hundred and thirty, during the time of James, the first Duke of Torringford, the mansion was heavily damaged by fire. Rather than attempt repairs, the duke commissioned a new structure, a stately home built in the classical revival style. It took seven years to build, and no expense was spared. Capability Brown himself designed the landscaping, including a small artificial lake and Temple Folly. The guidebook goes on at length to describe the grounds; shall I read that to you?"

"I would rather you not."

"It is said to be quite picturesque, although the author admits the descriptions are from the last century. Apparently the last duke was somewhat of a recluse, and it has been years since public visitors were allowed. Even Joseph Turner was denied permission to visit the grounds for the purposes of painting the lake."

So the old duke's incivility had extended to strangers as well as to his own kin. It was in keeping with what little Marcus knew of his character.

"We will have the opportunity to form our own opinions soon enough," Marcus said, hoping to put an end to this dry recitation of facts.

"True," Penelope said.

An uncomfortable silence descended once again, as Penelope appeared completely absorbed by the guidebook. She continued to read selected tidbits aloud, describing the towns they were passing through and other homes of note in the area. At last Marcus was reduced to feigning sleep to avoid listening to any more inanities.

That evening Marcus purchased the sporting papers, and the next day he buried himself within their pages, while Penelope continued her own reading. They spoke little, beyond a few stilted exchanges.

It was with a genuine sense of relief that they arrived at the Abbey on the afternoon of the fifth day.

As the carriage advanced along the drive, it climbed a slight rise, and then the trees gave way, offering a view of the Abbey. The prospect was magnificent, as the landscaper had no doubt intended. The gleaming white stone building had its reflection in the shimmering waters of the lake. Everything about the house and its surrounds spoke of careful design and calculation. It was impressive, and yet the overall feeling was one of coldness.

The servants must have been on watch for their arrival, for as the coach drew up to the portico, the servants began assembling on either side of the stairs. Swallowing nervously, he realized there must be fifty or more, each waiting to pass judgment on their new master and mistress. Used to Greenfields, with its handful of indoor servants, he wondered if he would ever become accustomed to such grandeur.

If Penelope found the presence of the massed servants daunting, she showed no signs. Instead she allowed a footman to help her out of the carriage, and then placed her left hand on Marcus's right arm as he escorted her.

A thin ruddy-faced man wearing a powdered white wig advanced to meet them. He was accompanied by a woman of storklike thinness, who wore a black dress and a white lace cap perched upon her severely swept-back hair.

"Your Grace, I am Mr. Gormley, butler here for these last dozen years. And this is my sister, Mrs.

Gormley, who has the honor to serve as house-keeper."

The family resemblance was unmistakable, both brother and sister being cursed with watery blue eyes and long thin noses. No doubt the "Mrs." was a courtesy title, in view of the sister's position.

"This is my wife, the Duchess of Torringford," Marcus said.

"An honor to make your acquaintance," Mr. Gormley said.

His sister repeated the sentiment, bobbing a brief curtsy.

"I thought you would like to meet the house-hold staff," Mr. Gormley said. "This is not all of them, of course, but rather those who could be spared from their duties."

His words were addressed to the duke, but it was Penelope who answered.

"That was most thoughtful of you," she said.

Marcus accompanied her as Mr. Gormley led them over to the left, where the menservants had lined up. Before they were halfway through the introduction his head was swimming, bemused by the names and descriptions of their duties. What on earth did a knife boy do, he wondered, and promptly missed the next introduction.

Penelope, however, showed no signs of confusion. She acknowledged each introduction with studied politeness.

Not all the servants appeared pleased to see them, but then that was to be expected. He and Penelope were unknown quantities, as it were, and the servants were naturally nervous. No doubt things would settle down once they realized that neither he nor Penelope had any intention of disrupting their routine.

After the introductions, Penelope dismissed the servants, and allowed Mrs. Gormley to show them to their rooms. The duke and duchess's apartments occupied the southern end of the second storey. Each had their own bedchamber and dressing room, which opened into a shared sitting area.

As he had instructed, all personal effects of the old duke had been cleared away. He wondered if they had been stored somewhere in the attics, or if the servants had taken advantage of his disinterest and earned extra pounds by selling them. Upon reflection he found he did not much care what they had done.

They dined that night in the formal dining room. It was not a success. The soup was cold and the joint overdone. Penelope questioned the footman who served them, only to be informed that the cook sent his apologies for being caught so unprepared.

"There is no reason for him to be unprepared. I sent word to expect our arrival today," Marcus said.

Penelope nodded. "I expect it was simply a difficulty in communication. Things are often set to sixes and sevens when a household changes masters. I will have a talk with the cook on the morrow, and set this right."

"If you like, I can speak to him," Marcus offered in a fit of generosity. Though he had not the faintest idea of what one would say to a recalcitrant cook. What if this was one of the fashionable tyrants who insisted on being addressed in French?

"No, this is my place," Penelope answered, much to his relief. "The sooner the servants know what to expect, the happier we will all be."

Now that they had reached the Abbey, Penelope half expected that Marcus would choose to claim his rights. Instead they spent another night sleeping chastely apart. She wondered bleakly if this was to be the pattern of their marriage. Perhaps there would be no children, after all.

She awoke with a headache, which was not eased when it took more than a quarter of an hour for a maid to respond to her summons. Finally the door was opened and the maid entered the room, bearing a pitcher of water.

The young woman's eyes went immediately to the bed, and Penelope blushed as she realized that the maid was looking for evidence of Marcus's presence. Apparently finding nothing of interest, the maid gave Penelope a smile of mock sympathy before crossing to the washbasin and setting the pitcher down.

"Nancy, is it not?" Penelope asked.

"Yes, ma'am," the maid replied. "Mrs. Gormley said I was to do for you, until you hired your own maid."

"Have you any experience at being a lady's maid?"

The maid shrugged. "I reckon I know what I need to know," she said, her eyes sweeping dismissively over Penelope.

Penelope wished she had thought to bring her own maid Jenna from Edinburgh. But Jenna was getting on in years, and it had seemed far kinder to let her remain behind, rather than dragging her on this journey.

She poured the water into the basin, noticing without surprise that it was nearly cold. It was a challenge, of a sorts, to see how she would react.

"You may lay out the yellow sprigged muslin," Penelope said. Cupping the water in her hands, she washed her face and then dried it on a linen towel.

After a moment the maid did her bidding, with the air of someone performing a favor. Idly Penelope wondered how Marcus was faring at the hands of the servants. Somehow she knew that he was not the kind of man to stand for insolence.

"I noticed yesterday that there are fewer maids than I would have expected, for a household of this size," Penelope said.

"There were more, but some of the girls left in these last days. Can't say I blame them, but it leaves me with twice as much work," Nancy complained.

"Your Grace," Penelope corrected.

"What?"

"It leaves me with twice as much work, Your

Grace," Penelope said firmly. "I see no reason to forget courtesy, do you?"

The maid's eyes flashed with rebellion. "Your Grace," she muttered.

Penelope completed her toilette in silence. Nancy's insolence was simply part of a larger problem, one that she had seen evidence of at last night's dinner. She should have expected this. No doubt the scandalous advertisement and news of Marcus's chosen bride would have been thoroughly discussed in the servants' hall.

A part of her sympathized with them. For all the servants knew, their new master was an eccentric fool, and their new mistress a brazen fortune hunter. No doubt the other maids had left because they were unwilling to work in such a scandalous household.

She understood, but that did not mean that she would accept such treatment. Indeed, if she let the servants continue on in their ways, it would seem a confirmation of her unworthiness. This petty rebellion must be nipped in the bud, and for that she would start not with a mere maid, but rather with the housekeeper Mrs. Gormley.

She breakfasted alone, having learned from a footman that Marcus had risen early and had ridden off with the bailiff to inspect the estate. After her meal she sent a maid to tell Mrs. Gormley that she wished to speak with her.

In a typical household, even without such a summons, the housekeeper would have waited upon her immediately after breakfast to review the day's menus and to receive any instructions. With a new mistress, Mrs. Gormley should have presented herself at once, offering to show Penelope her new home. But neither occurred, and after waiting impatiently in her sitting room for an hour, Penelope was tired of being played for a fool.

Finding the servants denied all knowledge of Mrs. Gormley's whereabouts, Penelope wandered through the great house. Twice she became lost as she worked her way through the public rooms, and finally down to the lower level, where she found Mrs. Gormley sitting at her ease in the kitchen, chatting cheerfully with the pastry cook, while a pair of kitchen maids scrubbed pans.

"Mrs. Gormley, I need to speak with you," she said.

"Yes?"

"Let us go to your office," Penelope said, nodding to indicate the presence of the cook and kitchen maids. "You may enjoy discussing your affairs in public, but I do not."

For a moment she thought the housekeeper would refuse, but then Mrs. Gormley arose. "If you insist," she said.

The housekeeper's office was just a few steps from the kitchen. A small writing desk with two chairs occupied the center of the room, while an upholstered chair sat next to the fireplace. Like the housekeeper herself, the room was austere, without any hint of decoration or frivolity.

Penelope glanced at the chairs, but decided not to sit. This would not take long.

Mrs. Gormley remained standing as well, her hands clasped in front of her, and her gaze fixed at some point over Penelope's shoulder.

"I think it best to begin as we mean to go on," Penelope said. "I wanted to take this opportunity to let you know what I expect of you."

"I have been running a duke's house for nigh unto a decade. I think I know what is expected of me," Mrs. Gormley said stiffly.

No doubt Mrs. Gormley was quite accustomed to having her own way in all things. The old duke had been infirm in his last years, and with no female relatives there would have been no one to challenge Mrs. Gormley's reign.

"I am certain the duke was satisfied with your service. But now you have a new mistress, and my expectations are a different matter," Penelope said.

"No doubt you will find this household a trifle grand, given your station. But I will endeavor to teach you what you need to know," Mrs. Gormley said loftily, as if condescending to a scullery maid.

Another young woman might have been cowed by such a tone, but Penelope had been running her own household for over three years now. And she had never been one to back down from a challenge.

"On the contrary, I am well versed in household management. As I am in the demands of courtesy and willing service. It is you, rather, that seems to have forgotten your place."

"Well, I never—"

"I understand that you have not been accustomed to close supervision," Penelope said, paying no heed to the housekeeper's protests. "Because the late duke led a retiring life, you and your staff have grown lax over these past years. I am here to tell you that all of this ends today. It ends now."

She took a deep breath and locked her gaze firmly on Mrs. Gormley's watery blue eyes. "Anyone who is not willing to stay in my service had best give their notice and leave today. Those who remain should be prepared to earn their living, and to pay me and my husband the respect that is due our position. Those who can not do so will be dismissed."

Mrs. Gormley's pale complexion turned even paler and her eyes widened in disbelief. "You can not do that, the duke will never allow it."

"On the contrary, my husband will abide by my decisions," Penelope said, wondering if this was indeed true. "Do not put me to the test, or the first persons I dismiss will be you and your brother. Am I understood?"

"Yes," Mrs. Gormley muttered.

"Yes, Your Grace," Penelope corrected.

"I understand, Your Grace," Mrs. Gormley said. "You will have no reason to complain of our service."

"Very good," Penelope said. "Then perhaps you will begin by showing me the menus you have planned for the rest of the week."

She spent the rest of the morning with the

housekeeper, revising the menus and then touring the house. Tomorrow she planned to inspect the household accounts, but she doubted she would find anything out of place. Mrs. Gormley was far too canny for that. Still she would bear careful watching.

Later that evening a footman came to ask her to join Marcus for a glass of wine in the library before dinner.

"I regret that I did not get a chance to see you earlier," Marcus said, as he handed her a glass of ruby red claret. "I hope your day was pleasant?"

"It was informative. And yours?"

"Busy," Marcus said. "I had no idea how much property the duke owned in Torringford. The bailiff Seth Hunter was able to show me scarcely half of it. But what I saw appeared well managed, I'll say that for the old duke."

"Pity he was not so strict with his household," Penelope said wryly.

Marcus raised one eyebrow. "Problems?"

"None that I could not deal with. Mrs. Gormley did question my authority, but I assured her that in household matters I spoke for both of us."

Marcus nodded. "Of course, you may do whatever you wish. I trust you will treat the servants fairly, but if there are those who do not meet your standards then feel free to dismiss them or pension them off as you see fit."

His reassurance gladdened her heart, for this had been the first real test of her authority. There was still much that they needed to work out between them, but his confidence in her made her feel that in time all things could be settled.

"I appreciate your faith in me," she said. "And I am certain that the household will settle down. After the gossip concerning that dratted advertisement, they had no idea what to expect."

"On the contrary, they should have known precisely what to expect. Did not my advertisement specifically mention I wanted a wife experienced in managing a large household?"

He grinned and she could not help laughing in response at the absurdity of it all. For the first time she saw the humor in the situation. They were still chuckling when the footman came to summon them to dinner.

EIGHT

They settled into a comfortable routine. Each morning Marcus withdrew to his study, and busied himself with the accounts and ledgers that were part and parcel of his inheritance. He kept up a brisk exchange of letters and instructions with his solicitor in Edinburgh, and the various stewards who oversaw the Torringford properties. In the afternoon he would sometimes join her for luncheon before finding some errand that took him out-of-doors. Penelope soon realized he was a country man at heart, far more comfortable talking with his field workers or riding the paths of the home woods than he was indoors.

They certainly made for an odd pair, the city-raised bluestocking and the athletic sportsman. She found herself curious about Marcus, who was so different from any other gentleman she knew, and used every opportunity to draw him out. To get to know him. In a way it was an odd courtship, where the couple grew to know each other after their marriage.

Marcus, she learned, was seldom given to talking about himself. Or to long speeches of any kind, although once started on his enthusiasms he could get carried away, until he realized from Penelope's glazed expression that he had lost her. But by dint of patient questioning, she had begun to form a picture of his character.

"Your morning was spent profitably I trust?" Penelope asked.

Marcus held the chair for her as she took her place at the table, and then took his own seat across from her. They had fallen into the habit of lunching in the small parlor, in part because it was smaller and less oppressive than the grand formal dining room where the old duke had been accustomed to take his meals. And the large windows offered a splendid view of the lake, which even on a gray and rain-soaked day was still an impressive sight.

"I will never get these ink stains off my fingers," Marcus said, holding up the offending hand and glaring at it critically. "I will be fit for nothing but a clerk, if this keeps up."

Indeed there was a faint stain on his first finger, and the beginning of a callous from gripping the pen. But this did nothing to detract from his hand, which was large and well shaped, though she could hardly tell him such.

"You should hire a secretary to assist you," Penelope said. "But until then I would be happy to help. I have a fair hand, and considerable practice, having scribed hundreds of letters on behalf of worthy causes over these years."

Marcus nodded. "I have a man who clerks for me at Greenfields, when need arises. But a duke's correspondence is far greater than a mere landowner's, and I refuse to become a slave to it. When I return home, I will see about hiring a secretary."

So he did not consider the Abbey his home, though by rights it was the duke's family seat. And yet, could she blame him? It was hard to imagine anyone cheerfully calling this enormous pile their home. As it was, the two of them rattled around like peas in an empty pod. It would take a large family to make this place feel like home.

"You will make your home at Greenfields?"

"Of course," Marcus said. "Though as you know I have asked McGregor to find us a place in Edinburgh, which will be yours. And I suppose we will need to visit here from time to time, to inspect the property and for the sake of appearances."

Such had been their agreement. She to live in the city, and he to live in the country. Each would get what they wanted, and would meet on formally arranged occasions. It was all very civilized, if a trifle cold-blooded.

He seemed to sense her mood had grown dark and sought to cheer her. "Although, one can imagine the Gormley's chagrin should I decide to make this my home. The two of us were uproarious enough; I dare not contemplate how they would react to the addition of a hundred hounds and their keepers to this establishment."

She had a sudden vision of a long line of coaches pulling up the driveway, and commencing to unload their precious cargo of beagle hounds, to the horror of the serving staff. Penelope chuckled, and Marcus's eyes twinkled in response.

"They would be suitably horrified," she agreed. "Nor do I believe that the beagles would enjoy their stay."

"There is that as well," Marcus agreed.

They finished the lunch in a companionable mood.

"Are there more letters to write? I would be happy to help you," Penelope said, glancing out the windows. The sullen skies had opened up and a heavy rain was now falling.

"No, I am done for the day. I am to meet Michaels at two," Marcus said, referring to the capable steward he had inherited along with the property.

"In this rain? It is a veritable deluge out there," Penelope said.

Marcus shrugged. "It is only water. We will not melt. And a rainy day is perfect. We can inspect the roofs of the outbuildings for leaks, or check the drainage pits."

She was absolutely certain that there was indeed no other duke in all of Scotland, or England for that matter, who would consider a rainy day as a perfect opportunity to inspect his properties for water damage. Then again, what did she know? Perhaps all countrymen were as mad to be out-of-doors as her husband.

"Go then," she said. "And stay dry."

"And you?" he asked.

"Have no worries about me. I have plenty to keep me busy, and if my occupations run out, there is always the library to explore. There is no friend on a rainy day like a good book."

Marcus shook his head in polite disbelief, and she realized that he found her as incomprehensible as she found him.

Indeed, Penelope had plenty to keep her busy, although she missed Edinburgh and the friends she had made there. Still there was the household to run, for despite her newfound spirit of cooperation, Mrs. Gormley bore careful watching. And after so many years as a bachelor household, there were a myriad of things to be set right. Not that she intended to reside at the Abbey permanently, but for appearances' sake she and Marcus would probably spend at least some time here each year, and she wanted them to be comfortable. Marcus had provided her a very generous household allowance, so as she toured each room of the house, she took careful note of the items that needed to be refurbished or repaired.

There was one room, however, that she did not know what to do with. The old nursery was set up on the top floor, and had not been used in decades. Now all it held was a dusty crib with two broken spindles, a battered dresser, and a wooden chest that held a moth-eaten rag doll and a spinning top.

"No doubt you will want this quickly set to

rights," Mrs. Gormley said, her eyes drifting toward Penelope's stomach as if she suspected Penelope was already pregnant. "Shall I send for the painters?"

"No," Penelope said.

"No?"

"No," Penelope said, instinctively loathing this barren and ugly room. "I see no reason to relegate the nursery to the inconvenience of the attics. There are plenty of spare bedrooms on the second floor. When the time comes I will fit one of them up as a nursery."

"As you wish, Your Grace," Mrs. Gormley said.

Of course there would be no need for a nursery, if their marriage was never consummated. And for that she was grateful. She felt barely adequate as a wife. She was not sure if she was ready to be a mother as well. Not yet, though someday she would have to face having children. After all, when she had agreed to marry the duke, there had been the unspoken expectation that Marcus would expect her to provide him with an heir. She had resigned herself to doing what was necessary, but her husband had yet to show any desire to fulfill his part.

If only there was someone she could talk to. She longed for Harriet Lawton's sage advice. But there was no one here, and so she pushed aside her troubled thoughts, and concentrated on those things where she could make a difference.

Four days after their arrival, Penelope was busy on the third floor, having discovered yet another chest of linens that needed to be inventoried. Dust flew everywhere as Betsy, the cheerful maid, pulled out the topmost stack of folded cloths.

"These are sheets. I think," Betsy said.

Indeed no doubt they had once been sheets of the finest white linen but time had turned them dull yellow and musty smelling. Not a surprise really, for the linen closets she had discovered had been in much the same state. Since the duke had few visitors and no wife to oversee the household, such niceties had long been overlooked.

She fingered the topmost sheet, and found that the cloth was still good.

"Put those in the basket for washing," she directed. Though no amount of bleaching would restore them to their pristine condition, it would be a shame to waste good fabric. "They can be used in the servants' quarters or as furniture covers if needed."

"Yes, ma'am," Betsy said. "There's a dozen, in all."

Penelope made a careful note on her inventory. "What's next?" she asked. Peering into the chest, she saw bundles of squares tied with ribbons. Napkins? Handkerchiefs? They would all have to be counted, she realized with a sigh.

Deliverance came in the form of a footman bearing a summons to join Marcus and a guest in the library, at her convenience.

"Betsy, please continue with the chest, and when finished in this room check the others in this wing," Penelope said. "Robby, would you ask Mrs. Gormley to come assist?"

There was a certain satisfaction in giving that order. Since Betsy could not write, Mrs. Gormley would have to take over the inventory, a task she should have done on her own these past years.

Penelope stopped by her chamber to brush her hair and wash the dust from her hands, and then went to the library.

As she opened the door, she saw Marcus speaking with an elderly gentleman dressed in an old-fashioned frock coat. Both men put down their sherry glasses and rose as she entered.

"May I introduce Mr. Abercrombie, the Vicar of Torringford? This is my wife, Lady Torringford," Marcus said.

"Your Grace, I am very pleased to make your acquaintance," Mr. Abercrombie said. With his white hair and kindly blue eyes he was the very embodiment of a country parson.

"I am pleased to make your acquaintance as well," Penelope said.

She took a seat and the two men resumed their own. She glanced at Marcus, but he seemed quite at ease, considering that Mr. Abercrombie was the first visitor they had had. She felt nervous, wondering how the vicar saw them. No doubt he knew of the circumstances of their wedding. Would he be shocked? Disapproving that they married in a civil ceremony? Or perhaps he was simply here to curry favor. No doubt his living was one of many that fell within the duke's patronage.

"Sherry?" Marcus asked. "I have asked the footman to bring tea, if you prefer."

"Tea will be lovely," she said. "The dust has left me quite parched."

"I must beg your pardon for intruding in this way," Mr. Abercrombie said. "I met your husband in the village, and when he mentioned that you were in residence, I am afraid I imposed upon him to make the introduction. I hope I did not interrupt anything of importance."

"You are most welcome," Penelope said. "And in truth, I am glad for an interruption. The linen inventory is necessary, but hardly diverting."

Mr. Abercrombie nodded. "It has been a long time since this house saw a woman's touch. The late duke was alone for many years, poor soul, and a bachelor household is simply not up to a woman's standards. Or so my daughter informs me, almost daily."

He smiled with self-deprecating humor, and she found herself warming to this kindly gentleman.

The footman arrived with the tea cart, and Penelope poured a cup for herself, and one for the vicar as well. Marcus elected to stay with sherry, and refilled his glass.

"So tell me, how do you find the countryside? Have you had a chance to view the neighborhood?" Mr. Abercrombie asked.

"It is quite a change from Edinburgh. What I have seen is lovely, though I have been so busy with the household affairs that I haven't set foot off the grounds since we arrived," Penelope said diplomatically.

Not to mention that she had no idea of how she would be received in the village. And as for the neighbors, etiquette dictated that they be the first to call upon her.

Until now they had had no callers. Perhaps the neighbors were simply being polite, allowing the newlyweds their privacy. Or perhaps they had already judged the new residents of the Abbey, and decided not to associate with such scandalous beings.

"I have no doubt that there are many who will be as eager as I to make your acquaintance," Mr. Abercrombie said. It was as if he could read her thoughts. "Tell me, will you be staying here long?"

"Our plans are not fixed, but we should be here through July at least," Marcus said, with a glance toward Penelope, who nodded. Such had been their agreement.

"Good, then you will be here for our summer festival. We hold it every year on the third Saturday in July. It is quite the event, with musicians from all over the county, mummers, games for the children and contests for the men. It is the highlight of the summer."

"I am sure it is quite the occasion," Penelope said. She found herself looking forward to the event with an almost childlike glee. Would there be Gypsies, she wondered? She was curious, having read accounts of country fairs, though of course she had never been to one.

"If we are still in residence, we will attend," Marcus said. He did not seem to share her excitement, but then having been raised in the country he had no doubt been to dozens of fairs in his time. It would not be a special treat for him, though as the landlord he would need to make an appearance.

They spent a pleasant half hour chatting with Mr. Abercrombie about the other diversions that were to be found in the county, and the personages she was likely to encounter. When the time came for the vicar to take his leave, she was surprised at how quickly the time had passed. Marcus walked the vicar to the door, and then returned to join her in the library.

"I thought that went well," Penelope said. "Mr. Abercrombie seems like a very pleasant gentleman."

"Pleasant and persuasive," Marcus said. "I met him in the village and before I knew it we were riding back here, so he could make your acquaintance."

"Well now we shall see if the rest of our neighbors are anxious to follow his lead," Penelope said. "Until then, I must return to my linens."

The corners of Marcus's mouth turned up. "Till this evening, then," he said.

Indeed, it was as if Mr. Abercrombie's visit was a signal to the rest, for starting the very next day the neighbors began to call. Some came out of curiosity, and seemed rather disappointed to find that Penelope was gently spoken and not given to wearing low-cut scarlet gowns. They were equally disappointed to find that Marcus was not the witless fool that the newspapers had painted him. Penelope bore their ill-bred curiosity with civil restraint, maintaining her composure as she deflected the most impertinent of questions.

By unspoken agreement Marcus and Penelope turned a deaf ear to all questions regarding how they had met, or the circumstances of their marriage. When asked, Marcus would merely reply that he was fortunate to have found Penelope, and change the subject. Penelope gave a similar answer. But even that was not enough to deflect the more persistent of their inquisitors.

After one particularly trying afternoon, Marcus breathed a sigh of relief when he was once again alone with his wife. Penelope watched through the window as a pony cart drove away with the last of this afternoon's visitors.

"There now, that's the last of them," she said. Returning to the sofa, she sat down and then lounged back, letting all her weariness show. "I vow I would rather inventory china and linens for the next two weeks than endure another afternoon like this one. Polite callers, indeed."

Marcus rose to the sideboard and poured himself a glass of Spanish wine. After a glance at his wife, he poured a second one, and carried it over to her. Penelope did not drink wine in the afternoon, but after entertaining callers for the last two hours surely she was as much in need of fortification as he was.

"Thank you," she said, taking a sip. She placed the wine on the table beside the sofa, and closed her eyes.

"I reckon there were half a dozen families represented here today," Marcus said. "By now we must have seen all of the gentry within an easy drive."

"I would not be so optimistic," Penelope said. "With our luck, there will be several more days of this. And then, of course, we must begin to return these calls. Out of courtesy, of course."

He had not thought of that. And naturally, most of the burden would fall on Penelope. As the Duchess of Torringford, her social duties were clearly defined. Everyone who had called was entitled to have Penelope pay them a visit in return. A gentleman, even a titled gentleman such as himself, had fewer demands placed upon him. He could allow Penelope to bear the burden of their social obligations, accepting only those invitations that interested him.

"Miss Pamela Abercrombie was quite pleasant," Penelope said, referring to the vicar's middle-aged daughter. "I will start my visits by paying a call upon her and her father."

If only all the neighbors were as pleasant as the Abercrombies, they would have few difficulties indeed. But that would be too much to expect, human nature being what it was. He was not even certain how his own neighbors would react, when faced with the reality of his marriage. Although they, at least, had the advantage of having known

Marcus since he was a boy. Here, in Torringford, both he and Penelope were very much unknown quantities.

"I am at your disposal, should you wish my company on these calls," he said in a fit of generosity. He knew he would be heartily bored by such expeditions, but it did not seem fair to allow Penelope to face the neighbors on her own.

Penelope smiled. "You are generous, but I will not impose upon your good nature." She thought for a moment, her brow wrinkling. "Except, perhaps, for the Snows. Miss Phoebe Snow was particularly vexing, and I can only imagine her four younger sisters are cut from the same cloth."

Indeed, Miss Phoebe Snow had been among the most impertinent of their callers. She had pestered Penelope for nearly a quarter hour, asking dozens of questions about Penelope's family and background. Eventually, seeing the tight set of Penelope's lips, and realizing that she was holding on to her temper by the slimmest of threads, Marcus had stepped in to rescue her, diverting Miss Snow's attention to himself.

"I will come with you to the Snows', and see the other daughters for myself," Marcus said. "And with luck, they will not let their envy overwhelm their good manners."

"Envy?"

"Could you not see it? Miss Snow was practically green with envy," he said.

"Of me?" Penelope asked incredulously.

He would never understand women. How could

she have missed something that was so obvious to him.

"Think of it," he said. "You are young, beautiful, titled, and with a fortune at your disposal. You have lived in Edinburgh where you are part of the most sophisticated circles of society. Of course she envies you. Miss Snow has probably never been outside the county in her life."

There was a faint color to her cheeks, and Penelope appeared suddenly fascinated with her glass of wine. "I had not thought of it in that way," she said, her eyes downcast.

"Then it is time you did," he said.

NINE

True to his word, Marcus accompanied Penelope as she visited the Snow family, who managed to display better manners than he had expected. He accompanied her on a few other calls, watching as Penelope's impeccable manners and natural charm managed to win over the ladies of the neighborhood.

He realized that in many ways it would have been easier for society to accept if he had married an actress or an opera dancer. Such misalliances were frowned upon, of course, but society knew how to behave when faced with such a couple. But there were simply no rules governing proper conduct toward a duke who had advertised for a wife as he might for a housekeeper, or toward the duchess who had presumably answered that advertisement. It was no wonder that the proper folk of the Lake District had no idea what to make of their new neighbors.

Gradually the curiosity seekers faded away, leaving only those souls who were genuinely prepared to welcome them into the neighborhood, and they began to receive a few invitations in return. They dined once at the Applebys', and Penelope took tea with Mr. Abercrombie's daughter Pamela. Marcus was invited to join Sir Harold Stevenson on a day of fishing, an outing he thoroughly enjoyed, while Penelope had luncheon with Lady Stevenson.

For her part, Penelope found country life pleasant enough, in its own way. And she knew that given time she and Marcus would become an accepted part of the country set. But she missed Edinburgh, with its intellectual atmosphere and the lively conversation of her friends. Here none of the ladies she had met admitted to reading poetry, although several had confessed to an addiction to romantic novels.

A month after their arrival, Marcus passed her the newspaper at breakfast one morning. She raised her eyebrows, for she had stopped reading the newspapers weeks ago, having no wish to read her own name in the society news.

"Page four, in the bottom left corner," Marcus said.

She looked at the masthead and saw that this was a two-day old copy of the *Edinburgh Courant*, which must have arrived along with yesterday's mail. Her eyes scanned down the columns, and then it leapt out at her.

Mr. Robert Carstairs is pleased to announce the engagement of his daughter Miss Amelia Carstairs

*to Mr. James Hastings, a gentleman of Edinburgh.
The couple plan to be married this autumn.*

She felt a hot flash of anger. Could James not have written to her, out of common courtesy? She was still his sister, his only living relative.

"I am certain they will be well suited," she said, after a moment's deliberation. Carefully she folded the newspaper and handed it back to her husband.

"So you approve of the match?"

"I think Miss Carstairs is precisely what my brother deserves," she said venomously.

Marcus nodded, placing the newspaper on the table. He took a sip of coffee. Then, in an apparent change of topic, he said, "You never did tell me who penned the response to the advertisement."

"No, I did not," she said. "Nor did you ever tell me how it managed to appear in the paper in the first place."

Marcus leaned back in his seat, the fingers of his right hand tapping idly on the table. "After learning that I had less than a month to be married, I confessed my difficulties to my brother. He and I drank rather more than was wise, and in a jest he suggested that I advertise for a wife, and wrote out the particulars."

He grimaced. "It would have remained nothing more than a poor joke, except the next morning rather than sending the advertisement for a kennel master to the paper, he sent in the jest instead.

By the time we realized the mistake, it was too late. The rest you know."

It made a strange sort of sense, and fit with what he had told her before. Marcus had implied that the advertisement had been written in jest, but the more she had learned of his character, the less likely it had seemed that he was the one who had done so.

It was time for some truths of her own. "As you have no doubt guessed, I recognized Miss Carstairs's handwriting on that letter. Though I do not know what she hoped to gain by penning it. The chances that you would choose my letter out of the hundreds you received were small indeed."

"It is lucky for me that I did," Marcus said. "I believe I may owe her my thanks."

"I think not," Penelope said tartly. "The minx needs no encouragement. It is enough for me to know that she will no doubt drive James miserable with her demands."

Echoes of their conversation stayed with him throughout the day. It lingered in the back of his mind, even as he wrote letters authorizing payment for his cousin's newly discovered debts, and later, when he was at Squire Turner's, inspecting the new drainage machinery with which the squire planned to turn acres of muddy swamp into productive fields.

He had been more than half serious when he declared himself indebted to Miss Carstairs. Without her meddling, he might never have found a bride who suited him half so well. In these past few weeks he had grown to count himself a lucky man. His new wife behaved as if she had been born to her rank. The household ran smoothly, and Penelope showed great refinement and tact in the face of impertinent questions from the curiosity seekers who came to call.

And most wondrous of all, he found that he genuinely liked Penelope. Superficially she was the kind of woman he never would have imagined himself attracted to, and yet the more he knew of her, the more he found to like. He had come to enjoy those hours he spent in her company. The tension of the early days of their marriage now seemed a distant memory, as they grew comfortable with one another. She listened patiently as he explained his plans for the estate, and offered intelligent suggestions of her own.

His only regret was that they had not consummated their marriage. And yet, having decided to wait until they grew to know one another, he now felt awkward. Perhaps it would have been easier to have had a true wedding night. Now, after these weeks had passed, what was he to do? Could he simply announce that he saw no reason to wait any longer? Or should he wait until the right moment occurred?

If that moment ever came, that is. She had shown no signs that she would welcome his attentions.

And there was another matter. This morning's

conversation had reminded him that the benefits of this marriage were very much one-sided. He had been the one in need of a bride to secure his inheritance. Penelope had been forced into this marriage by a conniving minx and a heartless brother. A brother who cared so little for his sister that he did not bother to inform her that he was to wed.

When he returned to Edinburgh, Marcus intended to pay a visit to James Hastings. It was time that Penelope's brother learned a few simple truths. Marcus had both wealth and position on his side, and he intended to use them to protect his wife. James and his intended bride would treat Penelope with the courtesy she deserved, or they would suffer the consequences.

But satisfying as such thoughts might be, they did not provide an answer to his dilemma. True, this marriage had been conceived as a marriage of convenience, but he had grown fond of Penelope. Was it possible that she had found her own share of contentment? He knew he was far from what she would have chosen for herself. Her tastes ran to intellectual pursuits, while he made no pretensions to great learning. Indeed he detested time spent in cities, and would far rather spend a day tramping through muddy country fields than to stay inside, with his nose buried in some musty tome. Yet, despite their differences they seemed to rub along well enough together.

And there was another factor to consider. The date they had set for their return to Edinburgh was fast approaching. If he was to woo his wife, he had little time left.

At dinner that evening, Penelope asked him to describe his visit to Squire Turner's.

"I found Squire Turner to be a most affable gentleman," Marcus said. "Indeed, he was so hospitable that I stayed far longer than I intended, and he seemed most disappointed that I would not stay to dine."

Unlike the gentlewomen of the county, their menfolk had been far more accepting of Marcus. Perhaps it was because he was now the most important landholder in the county. Or perhaps it was simply that they sensed in him a kindred spirit. After all, a few months ago he had been the same as any of them, occupied with the affairs of managing a small country estate.

"And the project he wished to show you?" Penelope asked, taking a spoonful of the clear fish soup.

"I was quite impressed. The squire has acquired mechanical pumps and has used them to drain acres of unproductive marsh, which will soon be ready for planting. Over one hundred acres so far has been reclaimed," Marcus said.

It was indeed an engineering marvel, one made possible by the latest in agricultural technology. A generation before such a project would have been ruinously expensive, if one had to rely upon laborers to man the pumps. Now, once the ditches were dug, each mechanical pump did the work of a dozen men laboring around the clock without rest.

"I have never seen the likes of those pumps. Of course in the highlands we do not have the same challenges with marshy ground that the land-owners here face," Marcus said. "I shall have to talk to Michaels about doing the same for the un-used lands near the Home Farm."

"It sounds most interesting. Perhaps someday I could see it for myself. Did you know that phy-sicians have observed an increase in ill health among those who dwell near marshes and swamps?"

Marcus shook his head. Penelope was proving quite a surprise, full of the oddest bits of knowl-edge. No doubt it had to do with her passion for learning in all forms.

"I recall an article by a Dr. Brown who theorized that the prevalence of sickness was caused by the miasma associated with such places. The squire is not only improving his land, but no doubt the health of his tenants will benefit as well," Penelope said.

"There is indeed much to be gained from ap-plying the latest scientific farming methods," Mar-cus said.

At Greenfields his efforts had been limited be-cause of the small size of his estate. But now, as a landowner with plenty of capital and holdings in four counties, he would have full scope to apply his talents to the improvement of his properties, not to mention well-trained stewards to carry out his wishes.

As the footman set out the main course, roasted lamb in curry sauce, Penelope shared her own news.

"We received more wedding gifts today," she said.

He nodded, taking another forkful of the richly spiced dish. Since their arrival they had received a number of gifts, a few from friends but many from strangers they had never heard of, acquaintances of the old duke perhaps, or simply those who wished to curry favor. There had been a truly ugly set of china, packages of linens and lace that Penelope, at least, seemed to appreciate, along with various curios and knickknacks.

His Uncle Quigley had sent a pair of shotguns from London's finest gunsmith. Not a typical wedding gift, but one that spoke of how well his uncle knew him.

He believed Penelope had received several sonnets composed in honor of their marriage, which had the advantage of being far more portable than the giant Grecian urn that his Aunt Fulton had sent.

"Was there anything of interest?" he asked, since she seemed to want a response.

"Do you know a Josiah Dickson?" she asked. "And is he a gentleman fond of playing jokes on others?"

"I know him, yes, but I would not say he is a

man given to jokes," Marcus said. "Why, what did he send us? Another urn? An insipid painting?"

"Nothing so ordinary, I'm afraid. When the gifts arrived, I was busy with the laundress. I told the footman to put them in the front parlor with the others." She smiled. "Imagine my shock when a quarter hour later the footman arrived to say that one of the gifts had just chewed the carpet Lady Muir had sent us."

He blinked, certain he had misheard. "Chewed?"

"Yes, chewed," she said. "It seems your friend Mr. Dickson had seen fit to send a half-dozen dogs for your kennel. By the time I arrived, five of them had escaped, and it took us two hours to round them all up."

"Beagles? Southern hounds?"

"I can not tell which breed, but the boy who brought them assured me that they were beagles. Five bitch puppies, and a year-old dog. Of Champion George's lineage, if that means anything to you."

It did indeed. "Champion George was a legend, and his litters breed true to his form. Truly, Mr. Dickson has been more than generous."

A gift of puppies from Champion George's line was a princely gift indeed. His own beagles were the smaller North Country breed, used most often as gun dogs. Until he had retired a few years ago, Josiah Dickson raised the larger Southern hounds, which were favored for hare hunting. Marcus had corresponded with Mr. Dickson over the past dozen years, forming a friendship. Often he had thought of experimenting with a cross of the two lines, to breed a heavier dog who could stand up to rougher country. Now, thanks to his friend's generosity, he could do so.

"Where did you put them? I should go see if they are all right," he said, pushing his chair back and preparing to rise.

"They are in the stables and you will do no such thing, Marcus," Penelope said with mock severity. "The servants already think that we are mad. Having you rush away from dinner to inspect your puppies will only confirm them in their opinion."

"Very well," he said, resuming his seat, although he could not repress his disappointment.

"Honestly, you are like a child," she said. "We must hope your own children show more patience."

It was the opening he had sought. He waited until the footmen had left the room, after clearing away the last course, and leaving him and Penelope with their tea, as had become their custom.

"We never did talk about children," Marcus said, gathering his courage in both hands.

"No, we did not," Penelope said softly.

"Do you want children?" Even as he asked the question, he wondered what he would do if she answered no.

"I suppose all women do," Penelope said, her eyes fixed firmly on the table.

"I can not speak for all men, but I know that I

would like a family of my own. A son, and perhaps a daughter."

Penelope lifted her gaze to his. "I do not claim to be an expert in these matters, but if we continue as we have, then there will be no children," she said. Her cheeks colored but she held his gaze firmly.

"Then perhaps we should change our ways," he said, feeling a tingling anticipation. "It would please me greatly if you would let me come to you tonight."

"I would like that," she whispered.

He rose, and gave a slight bow. "I will leave you, to give you time to make your preparations," he said.

"And so you can inspect the puppies," Penelope said, with a twinkle in her eye.

The puppies. Distracted by anticipation of what was to come, he had completely forgotten about the beagles that were awaiting his attention.

"Right. The puppies. It will do no harm to see that they are set for the night," he said.

TEN

There was such a thing as having too much time to think, Penelope decided. Perhaps it would have been better if Marcus had followed her to her bedchamber immediately, rather than giving her time to prepare.

But no, for then he would have witnessed her disrobing. It was bad enough that she had had to deal with Nancy's knowing smirks, as the maid helped ready her mistress for bed at this early hour. Having Marcus watch this would have been worse. Or heaven forbid, if he expected her help in undressing?

Her cheeks flamed, and as she brought her hands up to her face she felt their heat. She quelled the brief panicky impulse that made her want to run from this room. Instead, after a glance at the flimsy lawn that was her nightgown, she went to her wardrobe and pulled out a silk robe, and then wrapped that around her.

The heavy silk gave her a feeling of comfort, even as she chided herself for her foolishness. In a short while Marcus would see far more of her than was revealed by the lace nightgown.

It was at this moment that she most missed her mother. She had only the vaguest idea of what to expect. The day before her wedding, Mrs. Lawton had called upon her privately, and offered to explain the marriage duties. It had been an intensely awkward discussion, couched in vague generalities, and allusions toward doing one's duty. Rather than prolong their mutual embarrassment, Penelope had instead assured her mother's friend that she did indeed know what was expected, and Mrs. Lawton had seemed relieved to have the discussion cut short.

Not that she was entirely inexperienced. There had been those stolen kisses exchanged with Stephen Wolcott. Kisses that had been pleasant, and had left her vaguely yearning for something more. But before she could decide whether she would grant him further liberties, Stephen Wolcott had disappeared. And in the five years since, no other gentleman had stirred her feelings.

And there was the knowledge she had gleaned from the natural history tomes that she and Harriet had discovered in her father's library, and spent one afternoon giggling over. Not that she expected that knowledge to be of much use to her. After all, as creatures of reason, surely humans had evolved beyond the primitive instincts that governed the members of the animal kingdom.

Her thoughts chased themselves in circles as she

paced her chamber until she heard a rap on the door.

"Enter," she said, wincing as she heard her voice squeak.

Marcus stepped through the door, and her breath caught in her chest. He wore a silk robe of midnight blue, which exposed the strong column of his throat, and emphasized his broad shoulders. A quick glance revealed that his legs were bare, and her eyes quickly rose back to his face as she realized that he was naked under that robe.

Her heart began to beat furiously. Was she really ready for this?

Marcus crossed the room slowly, and the warmth of his gaze kindled a warmth within her.

"Has anyone ever told you how beautiful you are?" he said in a husky voice.

Penelope swallowed nervously. "I'm not, I mean I don't know, that is—" Her voice trailed off, as her mind went numb, overwhelmed by his sheer physical presence. She realized for the first time how very much had been hidden behind the elegantly tailored clothes.

"Hush," he said, bringing one finger up to stroke her lips. "There is no need for nervousness. We will take things as slowly as you wish."

"Yes," she breathed, her eyes fixed on the lush curves of his lips, wondering what they would feel like on hers.

He smiled, taking her hand in his, then bent his head down and kissed her. His lips were soft and warm, and she felt herself begin to tremble as his tongue gently stroked her. Her fears melted away under his skillful touch, and when he lifted his head, she gave a soft moan of disappointment.

"This is only the beginning," he promised her, and she found herself eagerly anticipating the other delights he had to teach her.

When Penelope awoke the next morning, she was alone in her bed. She had a vague memory of Marcus arising sometime earlier, kissing her on the cheek, and telling her to sleep as late as she wished.

Arising, she saw it was nearly ten o'clock. What must the servants be thinking, she wondered. No doubt everyone knew exactly what had transpired last night. Any embarrassment she might have felt was swept away in the warm glow of her memories. Marcus had been gentle and kind, and in hindsight her fears seemed those of a foolish girl. Not that she had experienced the miraculous transports that the poets wrote about. But though it had been shockingly intimate, it had been exciting and rather pleasant, until the brief moment of pain when she lost her maidenhead.

Marcus had assured her that once her body became accustomed to the act that she would experience even more pleasure. She found herself looking forward to seeing if he was right. She wondered if he would want to be with her again tonight. Certainly he had seemed to find his own pleasure in the act, if his lavish praise was any indication.

She rang for her maid, and instructed her that she wished to take a bath. Not even Nancy's knowing smiles could dampen her good humor.

When she saw Marcus that afternoon, she could not help the blush that stole over her face as she recalled the previous evening. But his manner was matter-of-fact, and the initial awkwardness soon passed.

After lunch, Marcus invited her to join him as he took his new hounds for a training walk. His invitation was diffident, but she accepted eagerly, curious to see this side of her husband.

After changing into a walking gown and sturdy boots, she met Marcus in the stable yard, where he was surrounded by what seemed a veritable swarm of hounds, and a tangle of leads. Penelope blinked, certain that there were more than the half-dozen hounds that had arrived yesterday.

"A trifle unruly, are they not?" she asked.

"It appears the journey has caused them to forget whatever training they may have had," he said, shaking his head, as one of the puppies began chewing on his right boot.

Standing aloofly apart from the scene, the older hound watched the puppies with an expression of disgust.

In a few moments, with the help of the newly named kennel boy, the leads were sorted out, with Marcus taking three of the puppies, and the kennel boy Sam taking the other two.

"Come," Marcus commanded, and they set off, Penelope walking beside him. One of the puppies tried to investigate her gown, but a sharp tug on her leash restored discipline.

The older hound followed at Marcus's heels, the picture of propriety. Clearly the antics of the young puppies distressed him, and from time to time he growled at them if they tried to stray too far from their course.

It was amazing how easily the puppies were distracted, and how difficult it was to keep the procession moving in an orderly fashion. She marveled at Marcus's patience, as he stopped for the sixth time to untangle one of the leads.

"How long does it take to train them to the lead?" Penelope asked. "Months?"

"Not long at all. A week, perhaps," Marcus said. "Today they are just high-spirited after their long confinement. And this place is new to them, so I dare not take them off leash. By tomorrow they will have worked off their excess energy and be better able to learn."

"They must be clever hounds indeed," Penelope said.

"Yes, well, the lead is only the beginning. Gun dogs work off lead, and need to be taught to follow their masters across all terrains, regardless of distractions. And to fetch game, of course." Marcus eyed the puppies. "I will probably breed these bitches rather than hunt with them, but they must be trained as strictly as any dog. If they do not have the heart for it, then there is no sense breeding them, for their puppies will also fail."

Marcus's face was animated as he expounded upon his favorite topic, and needed only the occasional comment from Penelope to encourage him. Really, in his way he was as passionate about his hounds as another man might be passionate about his politics or his poetry. It was an interesting glimpse into his character.

It took them nearly half an hour to cross the south lawn, the need to supervise the puppies slowing their progress to a crawl. As they began to head back toward the stables, Penelope noticed that the smallest of the puppies was beginning to lag behind the others.

"That one there is getting tired. The one with the white spot on her tail," Penelope said.

Marcus nodded. "See, she is smaller than her sisters," he pointed out.

Just then the small puppy stumbled over her lead, tangling her legs. She tried to stand but could not, and whined her frustration.

Penelope knelt down. "There, hold on, little one," she said. She unwrapped the leather lead from the puppy's front paws and was rewarded with a brief swipe of the puppy's tongue. The puppy stood up, then sat down again, panting.

"She's too tired," Penelope said.

"She'll be back in her kennel soon enough," Marcus said. He tugged at the leash, and the puppy obediently began to follow along with her sisters.

All was well for a few minutes, and then the puppy sat down, and refused to budge.

"I told you she was tired," Penelope said. "I think you should carry her."

"No, that will spoil her," Marcus replied.

"He's right, ma'am; you start carrying a dog and she'll never learn nohow," the kennel boy chimed in.

Marcus fixed the kennel boy with a firm stare.

"Begging your pardon, ma'am, Your Lordship."

"Please?" Penelope asked. "If you won't, then I will."

Marcus looked at her and sighed. "She's going to be spoiled," he repeated. But he was already reaching down, and he picked up the small creature, who settled happily into the crook of one arm.

"There now, princess, are you happy?" he asked the puppy.

"Completely," Penelope replied.

Marcus laughed. "Come now, let us take these puppies home before we lose all sense of discipline," he said.

On the third Saturday in July, Marcus had the pleasure of escorting Penelope to the village fete. Not even the cloudy day could put a damper on her enthusiasm, or that of the country folks for whom this was the major event of their year.

He watched bemusedly as Penelope strolled through the crowded streets, darting here and there as first one wonder then another caught her eye. She looked particularly fetching today, in a striped muslin gown, with a straw hat, and she collected her share of admiring glances. Indeed, unlike the gentry who had held reservations about the newcomers in their midst, the villagers welcomed their new duke and duchess with wholehearted enthusiasm, pleased to see that they did not consider themselves too grand to take part in such simple country pleasures.

And no one was enjoying themselves more than Penelope. She had never been to a country fair before, and she was determined to see everything. He followed her like a besotted swain, taking pleasure in her obvious enjoyment. Her eyes sparkled as she watched the mummers perform and opened wide with wonder at the fire-eaters. He bought her colored ribbons for her hair, as if she was an ordinary village lass, and was rewarded with a kiss on his cheek. When he offered to buy her a hundred more ribbons if she would reward him with another kiss, Penelope blushed but demurred, much to the peddler's disappointment.

Later Penelope joined Miss Abercrombie for tea under the shady elms, while he acted as an honorary judge for the boxing matches. What the participants lacked in skill they made up for in enthusiasm, and there were several loosened teeth and at least one black eye by the end of the matches. Fortunately it was all done in a good spirit, and no one was seriously injured.

As the twilight approached, Marcus made his

excuses, and went to collect his wife. He knew from his own experience that as dusk came the strong drink would be brought out, and the crowds would become rowdier. The presence of the duke and duchess would only be a damper on these festivities. It was best that Penelope leave now, for the sake of her own sensibilities as well as those of the villagers.

"Ladies," Marcus said, sweeping off his hat and bowing toward Miss Abercrombie, Mrs. Fulton, and Penelope, who sat in a semicircle, chatting. "I trust you are enjoying yourselves?"

"Very much so, Your Grace. And you?" Miss Abercrombie said.

"It has been a pleasant afternoon. And now, if you will allow me to steal her away from you, I believe it is time for Penelope and me to take our leave."

Mrs. Fulton nodded. "I think it is time I took my leave as well. Before the dancing starts."

Penelope rose. "Dancing?"

"Country dances," Marcus said.

"There are a pair of fiddlers from Little Moresby, and young Robby plays a tin flute," Miss Abercrombie explained. "Nothing fancy, but the villagers enjoy it well enough."

Penelope looked at him entreatingly as he took her hand to help her rise. "Can we? Please?"

He could deny her nothing when she looked at him like that. And the minx knew it.

"One dance. Just one," he said and put her hand on his arm.

He led her through the village, to the edge of the green. Indeed the dancing had already begun, and young couples galloped their way through what he assumed was a polka. Or perhaps a waltz. It was difficult to tell, for the fiddlers seemed to be playing two entirely different tunes, and the dancers had chosen to follow their own rhythms.

"The duke and his lady," a booming voice called out. He turned and recognized Bob Campbell, the burly innkeeper, standing next to an open keg of ale. "Come now, dance with us," he urged them.

The fiddlers scraped to a halt, and the couples on the green turned to stare at the latest distraction.

"Show us how they dance in the great city," one of the musicians urged, his face flushed with drink.

Marcus swallowed. He had imagined a quiet dance, not one where he and Penelope were the center of attention.

Penelope placed her left hand in his right hand. "Let us show them, shall we?"

He took a deep breath. It was only a dance. It was not as if there was anything to worry about. Nothing, that is, save the very real possibility that he would make a fool of himself in front of his tenants. And his wife.

"I make no guarantees for the tune," he cautioned her.

"Nor I for my footwork," Penelope said. With her free hand she twitched up her skirt, indicating the half boots she wore underneath. "It has been a long time since I danced in anything other than slippers."

Her smile was infectious, and he smiled in reply as he led her to the center of the green, the crowd parting around them. He put his left hand on her trim waist, and then nodded toward the fiddlers.

They began, in unison for a wonder, playing a tune called "The Bird in the Bush." As the flutist joined in, Marcus led Penelope in the first steps of a waltz.

The tune was lively, but Penelope kept pace, laughing at the occasional misstep. Soon other couples joined in. His own worries fell away, and he gave himself up to the enjoyment of holding her like this, watching her face flush with exertion, and her eyes glow with happiness.

This was their first dance, he realized, and the thought startled him so much that he lost his count entirely, and had to follow Penelope's lead for a measure till he regained his pace. And indeed, it was true that this was their first dance, though they had been married for nearly two months now. It was strange that he knew the woman he held in his arms intimately indeed, and yet he had never held her in the figures of the dance. There were so many firsts that they had yet to experience, and he found himself looking forward to new things that he could find to share with her.

As the dance drew to a close, he separated from Penelope with genuine reluctance. She curtsied to him, and he gave a formal bow, knee extended and hat sweeping his instep. This drew applause and cheers of encouragement from the spectators.

"Thank you, sir, for a lovely dance," Penelope said.

"The pleasure was mine," Marcus said. "And now, I think it is time we made our way home."

For he very much wanted to kiss Penelope, and only his sense of propriety kept him from throwing caution to the winds and doing just that. A gentleman did not kiss his wife in public, at a tenants' ball. Not when he had a perfectly good residence to take her to, where he could indulge the full range of his passions in private.

He gazed at her hotly, and Penelope flushed, seeming to guess his intentions. "Home it is," she agreed.

Penelope could not remember when she had ever been so happy. The weeks slipped by in a blissful haze, and Penelope treasured her growing closeness with Marcus. She found herself seeking out opportunities to be with her husband, one day joining him as he inspected the cottagers, and on another persuading him to take her on a picnic at the far end of the lake. She began looking at the countryside through his eyes, and found that it was not nearly so dull as she had imagined.

And then there were the nights he joined her in her bedchamber. True to his words, after recovering from her initial discomfort, she found genuine enjoyment in their coupling. And she knew that Marcus enjoyed himself as well.

Her world narrowed until it seemed all that mattered lay here within the walls of Torringford Abbey. Of course she knew it was too perfect to last. Still, when the end came, it was unexpected.

"This morning's post brought a letter from McGregor," Marcus told her one sunny afternoon as they strolled around the rose garden. "He has found a town house that suits our requirements."

The day that had begun so fine now seemed somewhat colder, and Penelope tightened her shawl around her shoulders.

"And where is it?" she asked.

"It is in Charlotte Square, in New Town. It was built for the Havens family; perhaps you know of it?"

Penelope shook her head. "No, I do not recall the name."

"It has been empty this past year, so he has arranged to hire a full staff to reopen the house, and bring it up to scratch. Subject to your approval, of course."

His deference to her wishes was pleasing. But of course, the house in Edinburgh was to be her residence. Marcus would be only an occasional visitor. It was as they had agreed, when discussing the terms of the marriage.

"I am certain that the house will be most suitable for our needs," Penelope said.

Indeed, it could hardly be anything else. Charlotte Square was one of Edinburgh's most fashionable areas, designed by no less a personage that Sir Robert Adam. It was a far cry from the modest circles that Penelope had moved in before her wedding.

"Will you wish to return to Edinburgh soon?" Penelope asked, though she was afraid she already knew the answer.

"I think that would be best," Marcus said. "We have already stayed here longer than I planned. And I am anxious to get back to Greenfields to see how it is faring in my absence."

She swallowed her disappointment. It was nothing more than they had agreed on. She would reside in Edinburgh, and Marcus would divide his time between his beloved Greenfields and the other properties he had inherited. She would see him when he visited Edinburgh for business, and no doubt they would spend the holidays together, for appearances' sake. But for the rest of the time she would be an independent woman.

"It will be good to see my friends," she said. "And I know you are anxious to see your brother again. Not to mention your beagles."

"Of course," Marcus said, although he appeared a trifle disappointed. "Then shall we set a date for our departure? Will Monday be convenient for you?"

Monday was just three days away. It was too soon, a part of her protested. But another part saw the wisdom of a speedy departure. There was no point in trying to hold on to a moment that had already passed.

"Monday will suit very well," she said. And she smiled brightly so he would see no trace of her reluctance, for such foolish sentiments had no place in the bargain they had made.

Marcus had lied to Penelope. The letter from McGregor had not arrived that morning. In fact it had arrived nearly a week ago. But he had hesitated to mention it, not wanting anything to disturb the fragile web of happiness that bound them together.

Much to his astonishment he found that this strange marriage had indeed brought him happiness. A most unlikely legacy, born from the old duke's meddling and the scheming of a jealous young woman. And indeed, not only had scandal drawn them together, but it had ensured that they would spend these weeks together in the seclusion of the countryside. At first he had regarded the weeks to be spent at Torringford as a distasteful chore. But as the days passed he found himself enjoying the time he spent with Penelope. Though she was clearly unused to country living, he admired the game spirit with which she entered into its pursuits.

And there was the pleasure of those nights he spent with her, teaching her the joys of physical love. He found her innocent enthusiasm to be a far more potent aphrodisiac than the practiced charms of his last mistress.

But in the end he could put off their return no

longer, and he mentioned McGregor's letter to her. He had half expected that she would make some objection to the scheme, perhaps asking that they spend the rest of the summer at the Abbey, or insist that he promise to bear her company in Edinburgh.

But she had done no such thing. Instead she smiled brightly, as if she had no other desire than to return to Edinburgh and to establish her new household there and take her place in society. No doubt while he had spent these last weeks wandering around in an enchanted haze, she had been longing to return to her friends in Edinburgh.

To be sure, he knew she enjoyed his company. But he knew she missed the busy whirl of Edinburgh, with its theaters, literary societies, and the companionship of her friends. Marcus was only one man, and he could not be expected to hold her interest indefinitely. No doubt in these weeks Penelope had already experienced more than her fill of country life. It was time for her to take her place in Edinburgh, where she belonged.

He scuffed at the ground with the toe of his boot.

"Is something wrong?" Penelope asked him.

He looked over at her. What could he say? That he was disappointed because she wished to return to Edinburgh? That he wanted her to need his presence as much as he needed hers? How could he admit to his anger? Penelope was behaving precisely as she ought. He was the one who had assured her that this was to be a marriage of convenience, and that she would be free to return to her own life in Edinburgh. It was not her fault that suddenly he wanted to change the terms of their agreement.

"No, there is nothing wrong," he said. "But if we are to leave on Monday then there is much I need to do. If you would excuse me, I will see about making the necessary arrangements."

"Very well, I will see you at dinner then," Penelope said. "Do not forgot that Mr. Abercrombie and his daughter are to dine with us this evening."

"I have not forgotten," he said, though that, too, was a lie.

So he was not even to have her to himself this evening. No matter, it was past time that he became used to sharing her attentions. And there was still tonight, and two more days, before they would leave this place, and he intended to take full advantage of these last days before they parted.

ELEVEN

The house at Charlotte Square was all any woman could have wished for. Mr. McGregor had negotiated a two-year lease, with an option for the duke to purchase the property outright at any time during the lease. And indeed she could see no reason why he would not wish to purchase the property. The address was respectable, the exterior of the house was pleasing to the eye, while inside the rooms were elegant and well proportioned. And owing to its newness, it held every modern convenience.

To Penelope's surprise, among the newly hired servants she found a familiar face. Mrs. Boylston, who had been housekeeper for her brother, and her parents before then, had chosen to follow her mistress into her new home. Under her keen eye the servants had polished and scrubbed every inch of her new residence. The presence of the housekeeper, along with her own maid, Jenna, provided a welcome note of familiarity in these strange surroundings.

The first few days after their return passed in a blur, as friends and acquaintances came to call, to pay their respects to the newly married couple. There were a few ill-bred comments from gossip-mongers, but in the weeks since their marriage other scandals had taken hold of the public's fancy, and Penelope felt confident that in time the novelty of her marriage would wear off, and she would be simply another accepted member of Edinburgh society.

Marcus was often busy with his affairs or closeted with the solicitor McGregor, but on most afternoons he did try to join her for tea, and she took a particular pleasure in introducing him to her friends. She would have liked to show him the city, but that was not possible. He stayed in Edinburgh with her for only a week before leaving to return to his home at Greenfields. He did not ask her to join him, and Penelope tried not to be too disappointed at the omission. At least he had promised to return to Edinburgh in the fall, once the hunting season was over. And it was not as if they were expected to live in each other's pockets. Such marriages existed only between the pages of romantic novels. Theirs was a civilized arrangement, where each party was free to pursue his or her own interests.

The day after his departure, Penelope was on her way to a luncheon when a footman came with the message that her brother had arrived. She instructed the footman to put her brother in the blue parlor, and then completed her toilette.

It was a quarter hour later when she entered the parlor to find her brother uneasily pacing to and fro.

"I hope my visit is not inconvenient," James said. He advanced toward her, as if to kiss her cheek, but she turned aside, offering him her hand instead.

"I am afraid I can only spare you a few minutes," Penelope said, taking a seat on the small sofa. "Lady Whilton is expecting me, and I would not want to make the countess wait."

It was no more than the truth, but it was also a subtle reminder that as Lady Torringford, Penelope now moved in a different level of society than she had as the mere Miss Hastings. Not that she had cut her old acquaintances, but rather that her social circle had expanded.

She eyed her brother critically. He seemed even stouter than she remembered, and his hair thinner. And his appearance, combined with his strict formal manners, made him seem far older than he was. Older than Marcus, though she knew for certain that James was five years Marcus's junior.

A most unprepossessing figure of a man, really, and she wondered what Miss Carstairs saw in him.

"I will not keep you," James said. "I merely came to offer my congratulations on your marriage. I can see for myself that this marriage agrees with you."

"Your consideration does you credit," Penelope said. James nodded, completely blind to the irony of her comments, and she wondered yet again how it was that she and her brother could be so completely unlike.

"And the duke your husband, he is well?"

"Marcus is very well indeed. He is at Greenfields presently, but I will convey your regards when I write to him."

She wondered what was behind this sudden interest in her welfare. Could it be that James felt guilt for his part in forcing her into this marriage? Not that she regretted it; indeed in many ways this was a blessing. But she saw no reason to share this knowledge with James. His callous disregard for her feelings still rankled her. Let him squirm with guilt. It was no more than he deserved.

Or was it that he now saw some advantage to himself in renewing their relationship? This was far more likely, particularly since it was now clear that society was prepared to accept its newest duchess, something which must gall both her brother and his fiancée. No doubt the social-climbing Miss Carstairs would very much like to move in the circles that were now open to Penelope.

"I see you are to be married yourself. I am certain Miss Amelia Carstairs will make an amiable bride," Penelope said.

James flushed. "I had meant to write you myself, but—"

"But I read the announcement in the newspaper instead," Penelope said sharply. "No matter. It is not as if we are close."

And yet I am the only family you have left, a part of

her wanted to scream. While another part wondered at how she could have been so blind to her brother's innate selfishness. She had completely misjudged his character.

"I would hope we could put this unpleasantness behind us, and make a fresh start. I know Miss Carstairs values your acquaintance and looks forward to knowing you as a sister."

Penelope's eyes narrowed as she searched her brother's face, but there was no sign of mockery. Apparently he was sincere in his belief that Miss Carstairs now desired Penelope's friendship, after all that had passed between them.

Perhaps she was not the only one who was blind to the flaws in those she loved. Or perhaps he was indeed telling the truth. Given time to reflect, no doubt even a simpleton such as Miss Carstairs would have realized the value in having a duchess as a sister-in-law.

"Miss Carstairs will find that my regard for her remains unchanged," Penelope said. Let James make of that as he would. She was not so lost to civility that she would insult her brother's fiancée to his face.

She rose to her feet, pulling on her gloves. "And now I must take my leave. Kindly give my regards to Miss Carstairs," Penelope said.

"I will," James replied.

The next day Penelope called upon the Lawtons. She could not help contrasting the warmth of their greetings with the stiff and awkward reunion with her brother. Mrs. Lawton joined Harriet and Penelope for luncheon, and then tactfully left the two young women alone, so they could converse privately.

"I can not tell you how much I missed the chance to have a comfortable coze. So much has happened in these past weeks, and there was no one I could speak with," Penelope said.

"I have missed you as well, although I had the advantage of Anne and Miss Gray, and indeed, our entire set to keep me occupied, while you were rusticating in the country," Harriet Lawton replied. "Tell me, was it as dull as I feared?"

"It was not dull, precisely," Penelope said. "That is for the most part the people were kind, if a trifle unsophisticated. And Marcus was most attentive."

"Indeed?" Harriet Lawton arched one delicate eyebrow. "I found him rather stiff in our meeting, although I will admit the circumstances were hardly ideal. I take it he improves upon acquaintance?"

Penelope hesitated, wondering what she could say. How could she explain her attraction to her husband, this stranger who had become her friend. They had few common interests, and yet, somehow, she had grown fond of him, and of his company.

"Marcus is a true gentleman. Kind, courteous, and quite intelligent, although our interests diverge," Penelope said. "I think we will find ourselves good friends, which is the best basis for a happy marriage."

"You sound as if you have reconciled yourself to this."

"I know we promised each other we would only marry for love," Penelope said, answering the unspoken criticism. "And indeed, if things had been different, I would most likely have remained a spinster. But as things are, I could have done far worse for a husband than Marcus Heywood. Far worse. He is not the man I would have chosen for myself, but perhaps that is part of his appeal."

Indeed, her own preference had been for pale and narrow-shouldered gentlemen of a poetic temperament. She could not have imagined herself with a tanned sportsman whose powerful physique made her feel so very feminine. And remembering what Marcus could do with his body—

"Penelope! You are blushing," Harriet Lawton cried. "You have fallen in love with him."

"No," Penelope said, shaking her head, but she could not meet her friend's eyes. "How could I?"

"But you are happy, are you not? Even though your husband has chosen to return to the country?"

"I am content," Harriet said. And it was true, although a part of her missed Marcus's presence and longed for the day when he would return.

"I am pleased to hear that," Harriet replied. "For there is one other bit of news I must share with you. At last week's poetry society meeting we

had an unexpected guest. An old acquaintance
has returned to Edinburgh."

"And this acquaintance is?"

"Mr. Wolcott."

Her heart gave an unexpected jump. Stephen?
Stephen had returned? But why now? There had
been no word of him for nearly five years and now
he came out of the blue. But where had he been
all this time? Was he still unmarried?

Penelope took a sip of her tea to cover her confusion. Once she had longed for this day, but now
it was too late. Two months too late, to be precise.
It did not matter if Stephen Wolcott was married
or if he remained a single gentleman. What mattered was that she was a married woman. A duchess no less. And she owed it to herself and to
Marcus to behave herself with all propriety. No
matter what feelings Stephen's return stirred up
within her.

"It will be pleasant to renew our acquaintance,"
Penelope said, aware that the silence had
stretched on too long. "Did Mr. Wolcott mention
where he has been?"

"I believe he has been traveling abroad."

"Then perhaps his journeys will have inspired
some great works. I look forward to hearing his
poetry," Penelope said.

"Is his poetry all that you missed? You were intimate friends, at one time."

"That was years ago, and I am certain that
Mr. Wolcott has forgotten all about that,"
Penelope said. He must have, or else why would

he have left her so abruptly, without once sending word? She had been reduced to scanning
the new arrivals at the bookstore and circulating
library, looking for his poetry, for some sign that
he was still alive. But there had been nothing,
and for a long time she had wondered if he
had met with an untimely death, perhaps a victim of illness or accident.

"You do not need to pretend with me. I know
you still have feelings for him," Harriet said.
"That is why I wanted to warn you."

"I thank you for your consideration, but I assure
you there is no need for worry," Penelope said.
"We will meet as old friends, nothing more."

Harriet eyed her suspiciously, but seemed content to let the matter rest. For now. "So, tell me,
what do you think of your brother's coming marriage?"

"I was surprised to read the announcement in
the *Gazette,*" Penelope said, gratefully accepting
the change of subject. "But I believe they are well
suited for each other. James called upon me yesterday, reminding me of his brotherly regard. And
letting me know how much Miss Carstairs desired
my friendship."

"A friend such as her you do not need."

Penelope laughed. "It is not my friendship that
she wants, but rather the pleasure of being able
to display a duchess to her friends and acquaintances that she wishes for. Still there is no need
to worry. I can deal with her pretensions."

"And Mr. Wolcott? Can you deal with his expectations as well?"

"Of course," Penelope said. And yet even as she said the words, she wondered if they were true.

TWELVE

Reginald welcomed him warmly upon his return to Greenfields, and insisted that he tour the kennels at once, to take note of the improvements that had been made. It was not until after dinner, when the brandy glasses were out, that Reginald turned the conversation to more personal matters.

"And your wife Penelope, she is well?"

"Yes," Marcus said. "And she seemed quite content when I left her in Edinburgh."

"She did not wish to accompany you? To see your childhood home, or to meet your neighbors?"

He would have brought her if she had shown the slightest desire to accompany him. But she had not. She was happy to be back in her beloved city. She did not need him.

"Penelope is busy getting the town house ready," Marcus said. "No doubt there will be time for such visits later."

Reginald nodded, his brown eyes softening with

understanding, which perversely made Marcus feel even worse.

"There is no need for pity," Marcus said. "I am quite well satisfied with how matters have arranged themselves."

"Of course."

"Penelope is a good woman. In time I am certain you will call her friend, as I do," Marcus said, driven by some perverse need to explain.

He did not want Reginald judging him. Did not want him to speculate on whatever was so lacking in Marcus's character that he could not capture the romantic interest of a woman. For surely the fault was his, having reached the age of thirty without ever finding a woman who looked at him with passion in her eyes. At least Penelope liked him, he was certain of that much. He had her friendship and respect, and they were compatible in bed. It was more than many couples had. It would be enough to build a marriage on.

"I look forward to getting to know her," Reginald said.

"You must come with us to the Abbey for the winter holidays," Marcus said. Though that was months away, and surely he would find some reason to see Penelope before that time.

"And now tell me, what do you think of the Southern hounds I acquired. Shall we mix them in with the others or try training them separately?" Marcus asked.

Reginald accepted the change of subject gracefully, and there was nothing more said on the subject of Penelope for the rest of the evening.

Marcus was glad to be back at Greenfields, and he made a point of telling himself so, at least once a day. What matter that his childhood home now seemed small in comparison with the magnificence of Torringford Abbey? Or that the pursuits which had once encompassed the whole of his interests now seemed oddly flat? The problem lay not in Greenfields, but rather in himself. He had been gone for nearly three months. It was only to be expected that it would take time to acclimate himself.

Not that Greenfields had suffered in his absence. On the contrary, it seemed his absence had hardly been noted. The crops had been planted, the roads repaired after the spring floods, and Bill Ferguson, the new kennel master, had done a fine job in training the new crop of puppies. For a man who had been used to considering himself indispensable, it was a humbling experience.

Not that they hadn't been pleased to see him. Especially Reginald, who had confided his growing attachment to a Miss Felicia Gillespie, who was visiting her cousins, the Dunnes, for the summer.

In the days that followed his return, Marcus gradually resumed his old routines. His neighbors extended warm greetings upon his return, and politely inquired as to when Penelope would be joining him. They seemed to take it for granted that she would wish to be with him, and there were nods of sympathetic understanding when he explained that Penelope was settled in their new town house in Edinburgh. Most of his friends seemed to regard his return to Greenfields as a visit, nothing more, assuming that he would naturally choose to call one of the duke's many residences his new home. He did not bother to contradict their assumptions. He did not need to explain his comings and goings to anyone. Except, perhaps, to his wife, should Penelope ever express an interest.

As the days passed, he found his thoughts turning more and more often toward Edinburgh, and toward his absent wife. He was surprised to find that he missed her company, missed the warmth of her smile, and the shy pleasure with which she welcomed him to their bed. He found himself storing up incidents to relate to her, only to realize that she was a hundred miles away.

They exchanged letters, of course. Formal, polite missives that held only a faint echo of the intimacy they had enjoyed at the Abbey, until he began to wonder if he had imagined that interlude. Had he really found in Penelope a companion? Or had their apparent closeness been simply due to their relative isolation and lack of distraction? Did she even think of him, now that she had returned to the world she shared with her friends? Her letters were full of her doings, lectures she had attended, plays she had seen, even an account of a ball to benefit the Peninsular Veterans Aid Society. Plainly she did not regret his absence.

At least one of his efforts had borne fruit. His

frank discussion with James Hastings seemed to have impressed upon that gentleman the error of his ways. Penelope had written of James's visit to her, and his desire for reconciliation. Although Penelope did not say so directly, he sensed she was still cautious over her brother's apparent change of heart. But publicly, at least, civility had been restored, and for that she was grateful. Of course she did not thank him, for she had no way of knowing of Marcus's role in this. Still that was as it should be. He had intervened not because he wanted her gratitude, but rather because it was right that he should do so. He was her husband, after all.

He threw himself back into his work with even more devotion, trying to convince himself that he still belonged here at Greenfields. And he wrote her equally stilted letters in return, not wishing to burden her with the ambivalence of his own feelings. Instead he described the arrival of the new South Country puppies, and how the one she had named Princess had turned out to be sweetly obedient, but far too fainthearted to be made a gun dog. He wrote of Reginald's courtship of Miss Gillespie, the unseasonable weather, and of other such matters, as he might to a casual acquaintance. And he wondered how long it would be before he found some pretext to return to Edinburgh.

The door to his study opened, and Reginald's face appeared. "Marcus, are you ready? Ferguson has been expecting you this past quarter hour, and it's not good for the dogs' discipline to keep them waiting idly."

Marcus glanced over at the wall clock and saw to his shock that it was nearly half past ten. He had been lost in his own musings, oblivious to the time.

"I can finish this later," Marcus said, laying the pen in its holder and recapping the inkwell. Lifting the parchment sheet in one hand, he blew on the ink softly to dry it, before placing the letter carefully in the center drawer of his desk. Then he rose.

"Another missive to the absent wife?" Reginald asked.

"A letter to McGregor, actually," Marcus said. He had written to Penelope earlier that morning. "Among our late cousin's interests are a mill in Lancaster and shares in a coal mine in Wales, both of which have been losing money. McGregor recommends selling off both enterprises, but I need more information before I make any decision."

"McGregor keeps you busy," Reginald observed. "Let us hope this tedium is soon finished with, and you can turn your attention where it belongs."

Marcus shrugged on his coat, and followed as Reginald led the way toward the side door. "Actually there are a number of decisions still to be made regarding the inheritance, and the final details of the marriage settlement to be worked out. I may need to travel to Edinburgh for a few days within the next fortnight."

Reginald stopped so abruptly that Marcus nearly walked into him. "Go to Edinburgh? Are you mad? The hunting season begins in two weeks. It's no time to go to the city, no matter that you've spent the past weeks mooning about the place like a lovesick fool. If you miss the girl so much, send for her to join you here."

"Perhaps one day when you yourself are married, you may presume to give me advice on how to conduct my marriage. Until then, you may keep your ill-advised opinions to yourself," Marcus said.

Reginald turned white. "I beg your pardon," he said stiffly. "I wished only to help."

The misery on Reginald's face made Marcus realize that he had spoken far more harshly than he had intended. He had no right to lash out at his brother in this manner.

"It is I who must beg your pardon. Forgive my rag manners, I am not myself these days," Marcus said, running his right hand through his hair, as he often did when thinking. "I am tired of answering the endless speculations of our neighbors, wondering when Penelope is to join me. Surely it ought to be apparent to everyone that ours is a marriage of convenience."

"And is that what you want?" Reginald asked.

"It is what we agreed upon," Marcus said. "And trust me, brother, I am not pining. I am well content with this state of affairs."

"Then we will speak no more of this," Reginald said, tactfully not pointing out that Marcus's behavior gave lie to his assertion of contentment.

Instead he changed the subject. "Come now, the dogs are waiting. I think you will be pleased with their progress, especially those from Rose's litter."

"Let us hope they do as well in the field as they have in the yard," Marcus said. "And I have my doubts about this tin whistle Ferguson has introduced. We never needed it before."

"Just wait until the dogs are in a crowded field and you will see the value of the whistle," Reginald replied. He began enthusing about the new training program, as Marcus had known he would.

For a moment it was as if the past months had never happened. He could pretend that he was still plain Marcus Heywood, a country gentleman, who had no greater concerns than a friendly disagreement with his brother over the best way to train the new hounds. But even as they fell into their familiar wrangling, his thoughts were never far from Penelope, and the impossible dilemma that was his marriage.

Penelope found that her new life was much like her old one. True, she no longer had to keep house for her brother, but now she had her own establishment to supervise. Her afternoons and evenings were filled with the diversions that she had enjoyed before, attending concerts, lectures, and of course, her favorite literary societies.

Although the frantic whirl of the Season was over, there were still a number of social gatherings, and hostesses who were pleased to include the

Duchess of Torringford among their guests. Not that she allowed such attentions to go to her head. But still, it was pleasant to make new acquaintances, and to discover among them those of a similar turn of mind, whose company she enjoyed.

But somehow, despite her greatly expanded social circle, her days seemed to be emptier than they had in the past. She threw herself into frantic activity, but still there was something missing. She did not know what it was, but she felt its loss in the quiet moments, when there was nothing to do but reflect, or to pour over the letters that Marcus had sent her, and pen her own carefully worded missives in return.

She could not explain this melancholy. Perhaps it was simply that she was not accustomed to living on her own, having spent her entire life first as a daughter and then as a sister. Or perhaps there was some other reason for her melancholy.

She tried to cheer herself by enumerating all the advantages of her new position. And indeed there were many. Marcus had been more than generous in the marriage settlements, and provided her with an extremely generous allowance as well. Not only could she indulge herself in the latest novels fresh from the presses, but she could also make material contributions to those societies and causes that she favored. Seeing her name on the list of benefactors of the Royal Astronomical Society gave her a real sense of satisfaction, and made her realize once again how indebted she was to Marcus. Indeed his absence was the only cloud on the horizon of her new happiness, and she found herself counting the days until she could expect to see him.

"Our own theater productions are every bit as fine as what one could see in London. Indeed, I found myself so enthralled that I was surprised when the lights came up at the end of the second act," Lady Whilton declared.

"The actors are very fine," Penelope agreed diplomatically. Never having been to London herself, she could not speak knowledgeably on the difference between the London and Scottish theaters. But it had been kind of Lady Whilton to invite Penelope to join her party, and the production of *Othello*, while not mesmerizing, was a pleasant diversion.

In addition to Penelope, the guests consisted of Lady Whilton's parents, Sir Archibald and Lady Harvey, along with Mr. Ian MacLeod. Lord Whilton was expected to join them for supper after the theater.

"I find the London theaters to be far superior," Sir Archibald Harvey said. "Which is only to be expected, as the city draws the finest actors in the realm."

"It is not the theaters that make London, it is the shopping," Lady Harvey said. "Next Season you really must go to London, Your Grace. You must insist that your husband bring you, when he goes to sit at Parliament."

Penelope blinked. She had not thought of this, but of course, as a duke Marcus would be expected to take his seat at the next session of Parliament. And if he was to be in London, perhaps he would not mind if she joined him there.

"I shall see," Penelope said. "There are many months between now and then."

"And, of course by then you may have reasons of your own for wishing to stay close to home. London will wait, but family will not," Lady Harvey said with a knowing smile.

Penelope blushed. Did Lady Harvey somehow know what Penelope herself was only beginning to suspect? Was there some physical sign of her condition, something that Lady Harvey's experience as a mother and a grandmother enabled her to read? Or was this a coincidence, based on the assumption that like any new bride Penelope would be expected to do her duty, and to provide her husband with an heir?

The door to their box opened, saving her from having to make any kind of reply. Penelope began to exchange polite greetings with their visitors, allowing Lady Whilton to introduce her to several of her friends. The box became quite crowded, and she was deep in conversation with Mrs. Anne Lawton, when she looked up to see a gentleman making a deep bow to her.

"I know it has been some years, but may I hope that you still remember me?" the gentleman asked with a smile. He took her hand in his, and raised it to his lips for a kiss.

Penelope shivered. He had changed since she had last seen him, but she would have known him anywhere. "Of course I remember you," she said.

She waited until he released her hand before turning to Lady Whilton. "Lady Whilton, may I present Mr. Stephen Wolcott, an old acquaintance? Edinburgh lost itself a poet of some note when he decided to leave our city."

Mr. Wolcott bowed over Lady Whilton's hand, though not as deeply as he had over Penelope's. "It is a pleasure to make your acquaintance, Lady Whilton," he said. "Any friend of Lady Torringford's must be counted a friend of mine."

"And what brings you back to our fair city?" Lady Whilton asked.

"The charming company, of course," Mr. Wolcott replied. "I have spent some years traveling the continent, only to realize that true beauty was to be found at home. And so I have returned, older and wiser, and able to appreciate all that I had left behind."

His words were directed at Lady Whilton, but Penelope knew that he was speaking to her. For her part, she could not take her eyes off him. Her heart was beating faster and her palms began to sweat. It was ridiculous. She was a married woman now. She had not seen Stephen Wolcott for over five years. She had had days to prepare herself for this encounter, ever since she had first learned of his return. She had thought that she could greet him calmly, as befitted a former acquaintance.

But she had not counted on the strength of her

feelings. When she looked at him, it was as if the past years melted away, and she was once again a girl of sixteen, in the throes of her first infatuation. It was beyond all reason and logic.

The theater lights began to dim. "Perhaps I may see you again," Mr. Wolcott said.

"Stay with us," Lady Whilton commanded. "There is an extra chair, and afterward you must join us for supper. Lady Torringford and I would enjoy hearing of your travels."

No. He must not stay. Already his mere presence had disordered her feelings. It was folly to encourage him to renew their acquaintance. She opened her mouth to object.

"Indeed you must join us," Penelope said, and was rewarded with another of his well-remembered smiles.

"As you wish," Mr. Wolcott replied.

THIRTEEN

As it turned out, there was no opportunity for Penelope to speak privately with Mr. Wolcott. As his hostess, Lady Whilton claimed the lion's share of his attention at the theater, and during the supper afterward he was in general demand, telling one anecdote after another of his travels. From his stories it seemed he had been traveling constantly over these past five years, visiting Italy, Greece, and more recently the Continent.

Conscious of their audience, her own questions were impersonal, giving no hint of the close friendship they had once shared. Had Mr. Wolcott encountered any personages of note? Did he share Byron's appreciation for the Greek isles? Did he find travel inspired his creative muse?

Her calm demeanor masked her inner turmoil. She did not ask any of the questions that had been burning inside her for the past years. Why had he left, without telling anyone of his plans? What had brought on this sudden urge for travel, when he had given every appearance that he was perfectly content with his life in Edinburgh? And the most burning question of all, how could he have left her, without so much as a word? They had pledged their undying affection toward each other, and then, without warning, he had disappeared, taking her heart with him.

His desertion had cut her to the quick, and she had vowed never to marry. And yet, a scant five years later, she was a married woman, a duchess no less, while Mr. Wolcott was the same as he had been. A few pounds heavier, perhaps, and his blond hair was thinner than it had been. But his voice had lost none of its magic, and his words still had the same power to compel.

She could not help wondering what would have happened if Mr. Wolcott had chosen to return this spring. Would there still have been a connection between them? Might she even now be Mrs. Stephen Wolcott, rather than the Duchess of Torringford? As quickly as the thought formed, she banished it. Such imaginings were folly, and made her feel disloyal toward Marcus. It did not matter what might have been. What was done was done, and it was up to her to make the best of things as they were.

The next Wednesday she had her customary at home for callers. After three hours of receiving visitors, she had just bid farewell to the last of them, when Mr. Wolcott was announced.

As he entered the drawing room, she took the opportunity to study him. The daylight revealed what the gaslights had hidden, that the years and constant travels had not been kind to him. Mr. Wolcott's once fair skin was now reddened, and his slender frame had grown soft with indulgence. Even his clothes, once impeccably tailored, now looked vaguely old-fashioned, as if they were relics from his wardrobe, or had been inexpertly tailored in foreign lands. She marveled for a moment that she had once thought him the epitome of male beauty.

And then he spoke, and the rich mellow tones of his voice banished all other thoughts from her mind.

"Lady Torringford, I hope I find you well," he said as he advanced into the room.

"I am quite fine," she said, allowing him to press her hand before indicating that he should take a seat opposite her. "And yourself?"

"As well as can be expected," Mr. Wolcott replied.

"I am afraid you just missed my other callers," Penelope said. "Mrs. Lawton was here earlier. You remember her, she was Miss Anne Cameron before her marriage to Roger Lawton?"

Stephen Wolcott nodded.

"Anne is now one of the patronesses of the Edinburgh Reading Society, and she mentioned that she would like you to come speak to their members, if you would be so kind," Penelope said.

"I would be honored, of course," Stephen said. "But you must forgive my presumption if I say that I am pleased to have found you alone. I have been hoping for an opportunity for private conversation. There are things that must be said."

"You had your chance five years ago," Penelope said. "Whatever needed to be said was said then."

She was proud of her composure. She had no intention of making a spectacle of herself, or allowing him to speak of matters best forgotten. Since their meeting at the theater, she had had several sleepless nights to resign herself to the knowledge that there could be nothing between them but casual friendship. It was up to her to set the tone of their new relationship.

Stephen Wolcott leaned forward, fixing his gaze on hers. "Five years ago I was a fool," he said. "I feel I must explain, although I know that I do not deserve your forgiveness."

"There is nothing to forgive," Penelope said. She would not reveal to him how much his actions had hurt her.

"On the contrary, I did you great wrong. I engaged your affections without once thinking of the consequences. It was only after I had fallen in love that I realized how impossible such a match would be. I had no prospects, no hope of caring for you as you deserved. And so I left Scotland."

She swallowed. Stephen had loved her. He had been in love with her. It had not been a schoolgirl fancy. If his words were to be believed, he had returned her affections in full measure. They were words she had once longed to hear, but now instead of happiness, they brought only regret.

"But why did you leave? Without even a word to me?"

Stephen glanced down at the floor, his face coloring in shame. "I knew it was impossible, and yet, I hoped, that is, I thought . . ."

"Yes?" she prompted.

"I went to speak with your father—"

Her father?

"He never spoke of this," she interrupted. Neither her mother nor father had ever hinted at such a thing, even as she moped around the house, wondering aloud what had happened to her former suitor. How could they have kept this from her?

"Yes, I went to see your father, to ask his permission to court you," Stephen said. "He made it clear to me how foolish my expectations were. He told me he would never consent to our marriage. I knew I could not stay in Edinburgh, where seeing you would be a constant torment. And so I made up my mind to leave."

"But why? Why would he forbid such a match?" She knew her parents had loved her, indeed they had indulged her in every way. And yet they had denied her this chance for true love. Without even a word of explanation. It was monstrous.

Stephen Wolcott shrugged. "I can not speak to all his reasons. We were both young, of course. And as a fourth son, my prospects were poor. I had hopes to someday support myself through my poetry, but my meager earnings were not enough to support a wife. Or a family."

"You should have spoken to me," Penelope said. "I know I could have convinced my father."

Given time she knew she could have made her father see sense. And then, how very different her life would have been. She would have been a wife, married to the man she loved, rather than wasting five years lost in regrets.

"I could not take such shameless advantage of you. I knew your father was right, I did not deserve you," Stephen Wolcott said. "And yet I knew I was weak. Were I to see you, to speak with you, I knew I would not be able to give you up. And so I took the craven's way, and left Edinburgh in order to protect you from our folly."

He had loved her. Enough so that he had sacrificed their love in order to protect her. It was a gesture worthy of the romantic hero that she had painted him in her youthful imagination.

And yet at the same time it made her angry, that he and her father had conspired between them to arrange her life, without once consulting her.

"You should have spoken with me," she repeated. "I deserved that consideration at least."

Somehow she knew Marcus would never have behaved in such a way. He would never have left without speaking to her, and asking her opinion. Never left her to sleepless nights of fretting and wondering. Marcus would never have broken her heart.

Then she realized that she was not being fair to Mr. Wolcott. She and Marcus rubbed along so well precisely because their marriage was based on friendship and respect. No doubt Mr. Wolcott would have behaved better, had not passion overwhelmed his good judgment.

He nodded. "I can see that, now," he said. "But back then, my pain was too great for clear thinking. In fact I have spent the past years wandering, trying very hard not to look back at what I had left behind. It was only when I learned of your marriage that I knew it was once again safe to return to Edinburgh."

It was some comfort to know that she was not the only one who had suffered. Stephen Wolcott had also spent the past years mired in regrets. At least she had had her family and friends, while he presumably had had no one to comfort him during his exile.

"And now that you have returned? Where does that leave us?"

"I can see I did the right thing. Your father was right, you would have been wasted on a mere poet such as myself. You are an ornament to the rank of duchess, and the Duke of Torringford is a lucky man indeed," Stephen said. He gave a wistful smile. "It is enough for me to see you happy, and to hope that we can remain friends."

"Friends," she echoed, wondering if such was indeed possible, given the strong feelings that had once existed between them. And still existed now, if her quickened pulse and queasy stomach were any indication.

"Of course, if you do not wish this, I would

abide by your decision and leave Edinburgh. Perhaps London would be far enough away, or there is always the Continent," he mused.

"No," she said quickly. "Scotland is your home, and I will not be the cause of driving you into exile for a second time. We are both civilized persons; surely it is possible for us to behave as friendly acquaintances."

"Nothing would please me more," Stephen said.

Later, after she had time to reflect, Penelope wondered if it had been wise to promise Mr. Wolcott her friendship. Would he really be satisfied with such a relationship? He had hinted that he was still in love with her. What if he wanted more from her, more than she was prepared to give? Perhaps it would have been better if they remained mere acquaintances.

But her doubts proved unfounded, for Mr. Wolcott behaved himself with strict propriety, as befitted a gentleman of such noble character. Soon she fell into the habit of accepting his escort to various entertainments. It was pleasant not to always have to rely upon the Lawtons and her other friends for such services. And his obvious pleasure in her company satisfied that part of her vanity that was piqued by her husband's continuing absence. Here, at least, was someone who preferred her company to that of his hounds.

But not everyone shared her pleasure in Mr.

Wolcott's return, as she learned one afternoon, as she accompanied Anne and Harriet Lawton to the mantua maker's.

Anne Lawton stood on a small stool, as the dressmaker's assistant pinned up the hem of a creamy peach gown, while Penelope and Harriet leafed through fashion books, eyeing the sketches of the latest French design.

"It is a shame the high-waisted gowns are no longer in vogue for evening wear," Harriet Lawton complained. "They were so slimming. These new Parisian styles show every pound and curve."

"Or lack of curves," Anne Lawton said with a laugh, gesturing toward her own rather flat chest. "Even tiers of Belgian lace and special undergarments can not make up for my lack of endowments."

"Nonsense," Penelope said. "You will look lovely in that gown; it suits your complexion perfectly."

"And my brother Roger is still besotted after all this time, so you need have no fears there," Harriet Lawton added.

Anne Lawton blushed delicately, and for a moment Penelope envied her. It was true, Roger Lawton did dote on his wife, and Anne Lawton returned his affection in full measure. Even after a year of marriage the two were nearly inseparable, much to the amusement of Edinburgh society.

The assistant rose, and walked slowly around Anne Lawton, viewing the dress critically. "There now, that's done it," she declared. "Let me help you off with that."

Anne Lawton was helped out of the gown and into a linen wrapper, and she took a seat on the small lounge opposite Penelope and Harriet.

"There are some bolts of new fabric from London that the mistress wants you to see. Let me bring this to the sewing room, and then I'll fetch them. And Mrs. White will be down directly with the crepe gown you had fitted last time," the assistant said, directing her last comment toward Penelope.

"So, have you found any designs to your liking?" Anne Lawton asked.

"This walking dress is rather fine, don't you think?" Harriet asked, handing over the sketch. "Perhaps in a sprigged muslin?"

"It is indeed fine, although with autumn approaching, I might suggest a heavier fabric. There is no sense in having a gown made that you can not wear until spring," Anne Lawton said. "And for you Penelope? Is there anything here that catches your eye?"

"No," Penelope said, shaking her head. "I indulged myself several weeks ago, and have no need to add to my wardrobe. Indeed, I only came today to ensure that the crepe gown was finished. I had hoped to wear it to the Hamptons' ball on Friday evening."

"And will you be joining our party?" Anne Lawton asked.

"No, Mr. Wolcott has offered to escort me."

"Hmm," Anne Lawton said with an unhappy frown.

Penelope looked up from the sketches to see Anne was wearing a frown. "Is there something wrong?"

"I have noticed that you often rely upon Mr. Wolcott as an escort these days," Anne Lawton said. "He seems to spend much time in your company."

"Mr. Wolcott is an old friend, and a pleasing companion. Why should I not enjoy his company?"

"It is one thing to enjoy his company. It is another to show a marked partiality to a gentleman who is not your husband," Anne Lawton said, in patient tones as if addressing a schoolgirl.

Penelope resented being called to task by one who was the same age as herself. "Are you questioning my morals? I assure you I have behaved with complete propriety. As has Mr. Wolcott."

"We know you are blameless. But in society it is appearances that matter, and your preference for Mr. Wolcott's company has been quite marked. If we can see it, others can as well, and they will begin to talk. And given the circumstances of your marriage, it is unwise to provide any fuel for the gossips' tongues."

Penelope was stunned. Harriet had been her friend since infancy. Of all people, she had expected Harriet would understand her. But instead Harriet had sided with her sister-in-law in mindlessly preaching propriety.

"It is precisely the circumstances of my marriage that make his companionship so welcome," Penelope said. "Unlike Roger, my husband does not crave my company. He and I have an arrangement, and I will abide by that. And if there are any explanations to be made, I will make them to Marcus. Not to you."

Anne Lawton opened her mouth to speak, but whatever she would have said was lost as Mrs. White opened the door to the sitting room, and her assistant followed carrying an armful of fabrics.

Penelope was still fuming during the carriage ride home from the dressmaker's. It was as if her friends no longer knew her, no longer trusted her character. Did they think marriage had changed her so much? That after living a blameless life, the acquisition of a husband and a title had somehow transformed Penelope into a jade? How dare they criticize her?

Her head was aching as she reached the town house, and after one look at her mistress, her maid Jenna tactfully drew the drapes closed against the afternoon sun, and offered to fetch a cup of soothing chamomile tea.

Slowly the tea worked its magic, easing her headache, and her fit of temper eased as well. She knew Anne and Harriet well enough to realize that they had acted out of the best of intentions. They did not wish to see her harmed in any way. It was unfortunate that they had begun espousing the most rigid ideas of propriety, but they were hardly to blame. If the situation had been reversed, Penelope might have found herself giving similar advice, urging a rigid adherence to the rules of society.

The circumstances of her marriage were unique, after all. It would take time for society to fully accept her. It was no wonder that her friends urged her to err on the side of caution.

But she was not one to let caution rule her life, nor would she live in fear of disapproving society matrons. She would show them that a gentlewoman of good character could have an intellectual friendship with a gentleman. In time even the worst of gossips would be forced to realize that there was nothing scandalous in their behavior.

With that in mind, she turned to the stacks of letters that had arrived in this morning's post. Among them was a note from Mr. Stephen Wolcott, offering his escort to Lady Swinburne's monthly poetry reading on Thursday. She had planned on attending by herself, there being no need for an escort to an afternoon function. But now, fueled by the remnants of her earlier pique, she changed her mind and dashed off a quick note of acceptance.

Thursday was a fine day indeed, as the city basked in the September sun, enjoying the warmth against the promise of the coming autumn. It seemed a shame to spend such a day indoors, and after spending the morning receiving callers, Penelope felt she deserved a reprieve. A stroll in the park, perhaps. It would not be the same as walking the gardens at the Abbey, but it would have to do.

Such plans were dashed when her maid reminded her that Mr. Wolcott was expected at three, to escort her to the poetry recital. And of course, it was too late for her to cancel the outing. With one last longing look at the bright sunshine, she allowed her maid to help her into her new violet afternoon gown.

Mr. Wolcott's eyes lit with admiration when he beheld her. "Lady Torringford, I vow you grow more beautiful each time I see you. And such an elegant gown; the other ladies will be gnashing their teeth in envy," he proclaimed.

Indeed Penelope felt very elegant in her new gown, which was made according to the latest Parisian style, a dark violet-colored bodice over a lighter sarsenet skirt, with no less than four rows of flounces.

"You flatter me, sir," she said. Indeed, she knew her own appearance was nothing out of the ordinary. It was the fashions that made a woman, as any modiste would tell you.

The footman nodded and then opened the door, signifying that Penelope's carriage was ready. Among the extravagant luxuries of her new position, Marcus had arranged for a carriage and horses to be stabled nearby so she would not have to rely upon hired coaches. Such was indeed a luxury in this crowded city, and thus it was her carriage that they used whenever Mr. Wolcott was her escort. It was simply a matter of common sense, really. No use in putting Mr. Wolcott to the expense of hiring a carriage, when she had one sitting idle.

Penelope allowed Mr. Wolcott to help her into the carriage, and then he climbed in. Rather than sitting across from her he took the seat next to her. She felt uncomfortable at his nearness, though that was indeed foolish. It was not as if his body was touching hers. The bench was wide enough that three people could sit here in perfect comfort.

Still, she wondered if it would be rude to ask him to change his seat. Or perhaps she should change her seat instead.

"Do you know who is reading today?" Penelope asked, seeking to distract herself in conversation.

Mr. Wolcott shrugged. "A new protégé of Lady Swinburne's, I believe. Nothing out of the ordinary I am afraid. And then, of course, no doubt some of her guests will wish to share their own compositions."

"Will you be reading?" It had been a long time since he had shared his poetry with her, or indeed with anyone that she knew of. And it was not for lack of interest. Upon several occasions he had been invited to read. She knew that Lady Swinburne had invited him, as had the Edinburgh Literary Society. Mr. Kenyon, the publisher of the *Scottish Review,* had urged Mr. Wolcott to submit his work for publication in the autumn issue of their journal, but the poet had demurred.

"No, I am afraid my epic is not yet ready to be shared," Mr. Wolcott said. He sighed soulfully. "My muse is fickle, and I am afraid my poor scribblings are unworthy of her inspiration. I have failed to capture the true epic grandeur that I so long to achieve."

How like him to disparage his talent. It was often thus with great artists.

"You are too harsh," Penelope said. "Could you but bring yourself to share your verses with a friend whose judgment you trust, you would soon learn that your fears are groundless. I remember well how gifted you were five years ago, and I am certain the passage of time has only served to strengthen that gift."

Indeed Penelope remembered Mr. Wolcott as a gifted poet, though she could not remember the details of any of his poems. Which was no reflection on his talent, but rather an indication of how hard she had tried to forget him when it seemed he had been lost to her forever. But even if she could not remember his poems, she remembered well the acclaim he had received at the time, and looked forward to hearing more of his works.

"You are kind. Perhaps, if it is not asking too much of your generosity, I could ask you to read the first quarto, and let me know your honest thoughts upon it."

"I would be honored."

Mr. Wolcott smiled, and took her hand in his, to express his gratitude. "Thank you."

Mr. Wolcott rubbed his chin with his free hand. "After waiting so long, I find I am anxious to hear your opinions. After Lady Swinburne's we could stop by my rooms, and you could peruse the quarto there."

"I am afraid that would not be wise," Penelope said, shaking her head. She withdrew her hand from his. "There are those who would see such a visit as a flagrant indiscretion, and such gossip would do neither of us any good."

"Of course," Mr. Wolcott said. "I should never have proposed such a thing. I am afraid I let my enthusiasm overwhelm my sense of propriety. Can you forgive me?"

"I have already done so," Penelope said. "We are friends, after all."

FOURTEEN

The library door swung open, and as Marcus looked up from his contemplation of the fire burning in the fireplace, Penelope entered.

"Marcus, I was so surprised when Andrews told me you were here. When did you arrive?" she asked.

Marcus rose as his wife crossed the distance that separated them. She took his hand in hers and kissed him lightly on the cheek. "You look well," she said. "I trust you had a good journey?"

"You look well yourself," he said, squeezing her hand a moment before releasing it. And indeed Penelope looked very fine, her eyes sparkling and her cheeks flushed with excitement. She smiled brightly, but he did not know if the smile was caused by his presence, or simply a remembrance of how she had spent her evening.

"You should have sent word to expect you," Penelope scolded. "I am sure the house was set at sixes and sevens by your arrival."

"It was a sudden decision to come," Marcus explained. "There seemed no point in sending a letter, when I would arrive before it did."

"You could have sent word when you arrived, and I would have come home at once," Penelope said, mock-scolding him. "Or better still, you could have joined us. It was only a birthday fete for Mrs. Lawton. I know she would have wished you to join us, if she had known you were in town."

The servants had been remarkably efficient, once they had gotten over their initial astonishment at his arrival. They had provided him with Penelope's whereabouts, seeming to think that he would wish to join her, or at the very least, to send a message for her to return home. But he did no such thing. Instead he had dined alone, and then sat in the library, quietly thinking as the hours passed, and his wife remained absent.

Marcus shook his head. "I did not want to be any trouble. And besides, I was somewhat weary from the journey, and thought it best that I not inflict my company upon others."

"How could you be any trouble? You, sir, are my husband," Penelope said. "We would have welcomed your presence."

We would have welcomed your presence, she had said. Not I. She did not speak of herself. And yet she did seem pleased to see him, although that was a small comfort when set against the dark thoughts of these last hours, and the strange restlessness that had prompted his journey.

"Was it a large gathering?" Marcus asked.

"No, it was just the family," Penelope said. "And myself, of course, although I suppose I count as family as much as anyone."

It sounded tame enough. And there had been no mention of a Mr. Wolcott, a name that had cropped up all too frequently in Penelope's letters of late. But still a niggling doubt remained. It was nearly midnight after all, surely a late hour from which to be returning from a small family gathering.

Unless, of course, she had been somewhere else. With someone else.

"Come now. I am fatigued and you must be as well. It is time we sought our beds," Penelope said.

He followed as she led the way up the stairs to the second floor. She paused at the door to his bedchamber.

"I am not that fatigued," he said.

She smiled and blushed. "I was hoping you would say that," she replied.

And as he led her into her bedchamber, he forced himself to set aside all of his self-doubts and petty fears, and gave himself over to the task of pleasing his wife, and allowing her to pleasure him in return.

The next morning over breakfast, Penelope again asked Marcus what had prompted his sudden journey to Edinburgh. Any hopes that he had missed her company were swiftly dashed when Marcus related that he had grown impatient with trying to sort out the late duke's affairs by correspondence. Instead he had decided to come to Edinburgh, where he could meet with the various solicitors and agents concerned, and settle matters himself. He planned to stay a fortnight, no more, and then return to Greenfields for the shooting season.

Whatever his reasons for coming, Penelope was pleased that he had come. Most of his days were spent tied up with his various advisors, so Penelope rearranged her schedule so she would be able to spend the evenings with Marcus. As word of his presence spread, invitations began to pour in. She refused most of them, but did manage to coax Marcus into attending the theater, and one afternoon he escorted her to a painting exhibition held at Hobson's Academy.

She had been pleased when he agreed to accompany her. She had given careful thought to this outing, searching for an activity that she hoped he would enjoy. The academy was showing an exhibition of landscapes and country scenes, which Robert Lawton had highly recommended.

But at first it seemed she had chosen unwisely. In the first gallery there were scenes of the hunt, and of gentlemen posed next to their hunters and dogs. She had thought Marcus would find these pleasing, but instead the pictures elicited only his scorn.

"Do you see that? The dog there stands half the size of the horse. No dog that size could run with the pack, or hope to keep up with the riders. It is ridiculous."

Penelope eyed the painting. True, the dog did seem a trifle large.

"I think the artist was trying to convey the beast's greatness of spirit by depicting him as larger than life," she observed.

"Hmph," Marcus said. "Greatness of spirit, my foot. More like the painter had no idea of what he was doing in the first place. And look at this other one he did. The horse's head is all wrong, and those legs are entirely out of proportion. It's a disgrace, it is. They shouldn't allow such work to hang in the halls." Marcus's voice was raised in outrage.

She could see heads turning to stare at them.

"Not everyone shares your expertise," Penelope said diplomatically. "Come now, surely there are other artists whose work will be more to your liking."

She tugged on his arm, and after a moment he followed.

The next room was no better, for it held numerous scenes of country life done in the style of Gainsborough. Even Penelope had to agree that the scenes were idealized beyond all recognition. The country folk were too rosy-cheeked, and too improbably happy at their labors, and golden sunshine streamed down from cloudless skies.

As they entered the third room, she was ready to concede defeat. Neither she nor Marcus were enjoying themselves, so there was no reason to stay.

This room was less crowded than the others, allowing a clear view of the paintings that filled each wall from floor to ceiling. A giant landscape dominated the whole of one wall, easily measuring a dozen feet across.

Marcus let go of her hand and crossed the room to stare in wonder at the canvas. She followed close behind, noticing her husband's rapt expression.

This canvas showed a broad river with high bluffs on either side, and dark green woods that stretched to the very limits of the canvas. To the west, the sun was slowly sinking into the woods. There was an overall sense of immensity and a lonely grandeur.

Penelope consulted her guide. This salon was dedicated to paintings from the New World, and the central work was a painting of the Hudson River and the forests of New York.

"Is this not marvelous?" Marcus asked.

"Yes," Penelope said. "It is called 'Sunset over the Hudson.' Painted by Mr. David Emerson during his travels in the New World."

Marcus nodded, his gaze still transfixed. "They say that in the New World there are forests that stretch for hundreds of miles, where no white man has ever set foot."

She heard the longing in his voice, and remembered her own youthful dreams of far-off places. Forests in England were tame things, managed by great landowners or held in trust for the Crown. There were no wild beasts to be feared, no native civilizations to be encountered, no great wonders waiting for someone to discover them.

"And would you like to journey there someday and see these sights with your own eyes?" she asked.

Marcus shook his head. "As a boy I thought of nothing else," he confessed. "But now I have put such foolish fancies behind."

It was a shame. "Surely, as a duke, you are entitled to do as you please. Even venture to the New World, if such is your desire."

Marcus turned toward her. "And would my intrepid duchess accompany me in my madness?"

He gave a smile of such warmth that she felt her bones turn to jelly. At that moment she would have promised him anything.

"Of course," she said. "I could hardly leave you alone. Who knows what mischief you would get into?"

"I shall remember your promise," he said.

The rest of the afternoon passed quite pleasantly, and they dined quietly at home, as had become their custom. Much to her surprise she found she was quite content with this domesticity. The constant round of social engagements she had been a part of before his arrival had begun to pall, and she was grateful for the respite.

And she was guiltily relieved to no longer require Mr. Wolcott's escort for social functions. Although at first he had seemed content with their

friendship, in recent days he had begun to hint
that he wished for a more intimate relationship
between them. Not that he had said so openly; it
was not that simple. Instead it was a matter of how
he looked at her, hand clasps that lasted longer
than appropriate, the way he stood just a trifle too
close. It made her uncomfortable, but as yet he
had committed no dishonor.

It had been a mistake to encourage his friendship, and to seek out his company so openly. But
his attentions had been a balm for her wounded
pride. Even when her friends pointed out the dan-
gers of such a relationship, their opposition had
only served to strengthen her resolve to prove that
a platonic friendship was indeed possible.

Perhaps it was indeed possible on her part, but
it was clear Mr. Wolcott still held warmer feelings
for her. She realized that she had been unfair to
him. In thinking only of herself, she had unwit-
tingly encouraged him in his devotion to her. Now
she would have to find a way to break off their
connection. It would be better for both of them
if she set him free to find a woman who could
return his love in full measure.

Yet, she could not break off the connection
abruptly, for doing so, now that Marcus had arrived in Edinburgh, might very well set off the gossip that she wished to avoid. With this thought in
mind, she added Mr. Wolcott's name to the guest
list of the dinner party she had planned. It was to
be a small gathering, barely two dozen in all. But
it would be an opportunity to repay the hospitality

she had received in these last weeks, as well as a
chance for Marcus to become familiar with her
new acquaintances. And including Mr. Wolcott on
the guest list should send a clear message to everyone that there was nothing between them but
friendship. Surely no one would imagine that she
could be so brazen as to invite her lover to dine
with her husband.

The day of the dinner party arrived, and
things began to go wrong from the moment she
woke up feeling headachy and slightly queasy.
Penelope dined on weak tea and toast in her
room, and after applying a cold compress to her
face, eventually managed to dress and make her
way downstairs to deal with the hundred and
one last-minute details.

The first to demand her attention was the chef,
who complained that the partridges were unfit for
serving. She inspected them briefly, clasping a
handkerchief over her face as the smell reawak-
ened her nausea, and backed hastily out of the
pantry. She agreed that game hens could be sub-
stituted instead, and the cook's assistant was sent
to the market to procure them.

After speaking with the housekeeper, she began
to copy out the menus, only to discover that Mrs.
Shields had sent word that she was too ill to attend. This made the party unbalanced, as Mrs.
Shields had been invited to partner Mr. Wolcott.
After much frantic thinking Penelope sent a message to Miss Boyle, who was kindhearted enough
to agree to the last-minute invitation.

By the time the guests began arriving, Penelope
was exhausted. Even Marcus's compliments on her
appearance did little to restore her spirits. She
could not understand why she was so tired. She
had hosted parties many times before, and far
larger gatherings. Perhaps it was simply that this
was the first time she had held such a gathering
in the new town house. Or perhaps it was simply
that she wanted every detail of this evening to be
perfect, even if she herself found little pleasure in
the event.

The dinner was a success, or at least her guests
seemed to think so. The conversation was lively,
and though she could not hear Marcus's conversation from her end of the table, he seemed to be
holding his own as he spoke with Lord Whilton
and Roger Lawton. Lord Whilton was a sportsman
of some note, and he and Marcus seemed to be
kindred spirits.

After dinner, Penelope led the ladies to the
drawing room, where they sipped tea and gossiped
until joined by the gentlemen. As often happens
at such gatherings, the guests broke into small
groups. A few of the gentlemen stood with Marcus,
discussing the prospects for the shooting season,
while others clustered discussing politics or literature, and Miss Boyle related a humorous tale of
her encounter in the park with the Earl of Ellicott,
whom she had mistaken for her cousin.

Penelope circulated among her guests, dis-
creetly checking on the refreshments, and offering her opinion when asked. But she did not allow

herself to be drawn into any one conversation. Instead, she suppressed a yawn, and wondered somewhat guiltily if it was beyond all measure of politeness to chivvy her guests to leave at this early hour.

A footman approached and caught her eye. "Mr. Campbell would like to speak with you," he said.

Penelope made her excuses and left the drawing room. She found Mr. Campbell emerging from the door that led down to the cellars.

"Your Grace, John informed me that the port was running low, so I took it upon myself to bring up two more bottles to be decanted," Mr. Campbell said, handing the bottles over to the waiting footman. "Will you be wanting more champagne poured as well?"

"No," Penelope said after a moment's thought. "I doubt we will drink half of what has been opened. The ladies seem to prefer the chilled Madeira this evening."

And perhaps if they ran out of champagne, the guests would be encouraged to leave soon, and Penelope could seek out her own bed. It was an unworthy thought, but her earlier headache had returned in full force.

"Very well, Your Grace," the butler replied.

As Penelope made her way back down the hall, she found Mr. Wolcott standing outside the door to the drawing room.

"Sir?" she asked, wondering at his presence.

"I hoped I might have a word with you," Mr. Wolcott said. "In private."

Penelope hesitated. She was tired, her head ached, and if she was absent for much longer her guests would begin to wonder.

"Please," he entreated, reaching for her hand.

She pulled her hand back before he could clasp it.

"As you wish. I can spare a moment," she said.

She led him to the small parlor that she had taken for her own. Mr. Wolcott closed the door behind them, a breach of propriety. She thought about asking him to reopen it, and then realized that perhaps it was best that there be no witnesses to this conversation.

"Have I done something to offend you?" Mr. Wolcott asked.

"No," Penelope said.

"Then why this sudden coldness? You have scarcely spoken to me this past fortnight," Mr. Wolcott said. "Please, tell me what I have done wrong and I will mend my ways."

"I have been otherwise occupied since my husband journeyed to Edinburgh," Penelope said.

Mr. Wolcott nodded, rubbing his chin thoughtfully. "I hear he is soon to depart. May I hope for your companionship once he has returned to his muddy fields and yapping dogs?"

"Marcus's stay is undetermined," Penelope said. It was only a small prevarication. True, Marcus had said he only intended to stay a fortnight, but it had been that long already, and he showed no signs of leaving.

"But surely you can not prefer his company to mine? He is scarcely civilized, for all his newly acquired rank and wealth. I doubt he's read a dozen books in his entire life. What on earth do you find in common with him?"

Penelope grew angry. How dare he disparage Marcus in this way? "My husband is a true gentleman. Just because he sees no need to prattle does not reflect upon his intelligence or his character. Indeed, I find I prefer his company above all others," she said, realizing even as she said it that it was the truth. "In fact it is our differences that strengthen our bond."

"I apologize if I misspoke," Mr. Wolcott said, seemingly realizing that he had erred. "I did not mean to insult the duke. I am certain that in his own way he is a man of worth. It was simply my disappointment speaking. In these past weeks I had allowed myself to hope—"

"That is my fault," Penelope interrupted. She had a strong suspicion as to what Mr. Wolcott had hoped for, but did not wish to hear the words said aloud. "I have been unfair to you, taking advantage of your good nature when there can be nothing but civilized friendship between us. In fact I believe it for the best that we not see each other in the future, to avoid any awkwardness."

There. She had said it. She had expected to feel sorrow, but instead she felt an overwhelming sense of relief. It was hard to realize that she had once thought herself passionately in love with this man. Now all she felt was a distant affection, tinged with regret.

"And there is no chance I can change your mind?"

"None," she said firmly.

Mr. Wolcott eyed her assessingly. "I believe you," he said. And then he smiled, and it was not a pleasant expression. "Which is unfortunate for you."

"I beg your pardon?"

Mr. Wolcott advanced toward her, and Penelope retreated until she found her back literally against the wall.

"Do you know how much blunt it takes to live as a gentleman? To support myself as I deserve? Far more than the measly allowance my father sends me, and a hundred times more than I will ever make from that pathetic drivel I pass off as poetry."

His blue eyes were cold, and his face had hardened. Penelope realized for the first time that she was seeing the true man behind the civilized mask that he showed the rest of the world. She was frightened, although as yet he had made no move to touch her.

If he did, she would have to call for help, regardless of the consequences to her reputation. She closed her eyes in mortification. How could she have been so foolish as to agree to this private meeting? Were she to be discovered, the scandal would undo all the hard work she had done to reclaim her good name. A duchess found privately entertaining one of her male guests. Her reputation would be ruined, and the blame would be hers for having allowed herself to be placed in this situation.

"I do not understand you," Penelope said.

"Did you never guess why I left Edinburgh? Your father paid me quite handsomely to do so," Mr. Wolcott said. "He would have done anything to protect his precious daughter."

Penelope swallowed, tasting bile.

"Other papas in London were equally protective of their daughters," Mr. Wolcott said, his eyes lost in some private meditation. "Of course, once my reputation was known, it was time to take my earnings and leave the country. On the Continent one can live quite well on a modest sum. I did travel, as I had said. But eventually the money ran low, and I returned to England. Imagine my surprise when I found out that you had just become a wealthy duchess. I knew my fortune was made."

"You thought I would pay you off?"

Mr. Wolcott shrugged. "I hoped you would agree to be my patroness. By all accounts your husband was a dull stick, and I thought you would be pleased to take a lover who shared your interests. And once I had made you mine, it would be a simple matter to convince you to share your wealth. To support my muse, as it were. How could I know that you would actually be loyal to that clod?"

Penelope raised her hand to slap him, but he caught it tightly within his fist.

"Temper, temper," he said. "Think well before you do something you will regret. Would you like me to call out and summon the servants?"

"No," Penelope said swiftly. There was no need for anyone else to witness her humiliation.

"I thought not," he said, with an unpleasant smirk. "I will make this simple for you. Let history repeat itself. You will give me five thousand pounds, and I will disappear from Scotland, and trouble you no more."

"I will do no such thing," Penelope said.

"I advise you not to be foolish," Mr. Wolcott said. "If you do not cooperate, I will make sure all of Edinburgh hears that we have been lovers. And then you will find out just how tolerant your husband is."

"You are despicable," Penelope said.

Mr. Wolcott shook his head. "Merely practical. The choice is yours. I will expect your answer tomorrow. You have my direction."

With that he released her hand and stepped back. He gave an ironic bow and then left.

Penelope sank down in a chair, her nerves overcome by that confrontation. She felt like such a fool. How could she ever have been taken in by such a man? Many had tried to warn her, but she had been too blind to see.

She was ashamed that she had fallen for his wiles not once but twice. And this time she was not a girl of sixteen, but a married woman of one-and-twenty. She should have known better. If only her father had told her of Mr. Wolcott's perfidy, he would never have had had a chance to inveigle himself into her life again. But it was not really her father's fault. He had been trying to protect her. Perhaps he would have told her when she was older, but he had died without ever having told her what he had done. And so she had spent five years cherishing the illusion of her one great love, only to now discover that it had been just that. An illusion. Mr. Wolcott had never loved her. He had never loved anyone but himself.

And she? She had realized some days ago that she was not in love with Mr. Wolcott. Indeed his constant attentions and flatteries had begun to feel oppressive and cloying. Not to mention that his behavior of late had made her uncomfortable. While he had continued to behave with propriety, there was something in his glances, in his sighs, in the way he always seemed to be standing so close that she could hardly breathe.

In fact, the more she grew to know Mr. Wolcott, the more she realized that she had never really known him at all. Her feelings for him were nothing but the echo of the infatuation that a young woman had felt toward the first man who had paid her court. Her vanity, wounded by Marcus's desertion to the countryside, had taken great pleasure in having such a devoted follower. Here was a man who had loved her, a man who had gone into exile sim-

ply because he could not have her. What more
proof could she need that here was the romantic hero that she had long desired?

But it had all been a delusion. She had been in
love with the idea of being in love. Mr. Wolcott
was simply the object she had fixed upon, project-
ing all her hopes and fancies upon him.

If not for Marcus, she might never have known
what it was to love a flesh-and-blood man, rather
than a dream image she had created in her mind.
Only then had she been able to see how shallow
her feelings for Mr. Wolcott were.

But even then, knowing that she did not love
Mr. Wolcott, she had still taken pity on him, be-
lieving that he was in love with her. She had wor-
ried over how he would take the news that they
could not be friends. Never could she have imagined his perfidy.

Now she had to face the fact that she had been
a fool. By encouraging Mr. Wolcott, she had given
the gossips new fuel for scandal. And since she
had no intention of giving in to Mr. Wolcott's demands, she would have to face the consequences.
She no longer doubted that Mr. Wolcott would do
exactly as he promised, and try to blacken her
name.

Penelope gave a mirthless laugh. To think that
she had once considered herself a fine judge of
character. And yet she had completely misjudged
both her brother and Mr. Wolcott.

She hoped that she was better at reading Marcus's character. If there was any hope for them to

build a true marriage, she would have to go to him, and tell him everything. And then hope that he could find it in his heart to forgive her.

FIFTEEN

Marcus normally dreaded social gatherings composed of strangers, but to his own surprise he found himself enjoying the dinner party and his role as host. It helped that most of the guests were not strangers. Penelope had taken great care in the guest list, ensuring he would have someone to talk with by inviting two of his friends, Samuel Curran and Josiah Barrett, along with their wives. And he had met most of the rest of the guests at one social function or another. Indeed it could be said that the Lawton women ran tame in his house, as Penelope did in theirs. There were only two persons present whom he had never met before, the amiable and utterly forgettable Miss Boyle, and the poet Stephen Wolcott.

Mr. Wolcott's name had cropped up frequently in Penelope's letters, and so Marcus had taken the opportunity to study him carefully. But after several hours in the gentleman's company he could not understand what Penelope saw in this man. And indeed she did not seem to be alone in her admiration, for many of the ladies present seemed enraptured by the poet, who preened under their attentions.

Could they not see that this man was nothing but a vain poseur? He had no conversation save flattery and the telling of self-aggrandizing stories. And as for his poetry, Marcus wagered it was as shallow as the man himself. No doubt Penelope had realized his lack of worth herself, and this explained her seeming indifference to her guest.

Obscurely comforted by this revelation, he conversed animatedly with Lord Whilton about the upcoming shooting season, pleased to find a fellow sportsman among this company. But a part of his attention was fixed on Penelope, and he noticed when a footman came to speak with her, and she followed him from the drawing room.

His eyes narrowed as a few moments later Mr. Wolcott left the room as well. As the minutes passed, and neither Penelope nor Mr. Wolcott returned, his concern began to grow. It looked less and less like a coincidence and more as if his wife was keeping an assignation. And yet that was impossible. She had two dozen guests who could be expected to notice her absence at any moment.

He waited another five minutes, until his patience snapped. Making his excuses to Lord Whilton, he made his way through the crowd, pausing to answer a question raised by Josiah Barrett. It would not do for anyone to suspect that he was upset. As he neared the door, it opened, and Mr. Wolcott entered. Alone. His eyes caught Marcus's and he gave an affable nod. There was nothing in his dress or demeanor to indicate that anything illicit or untoward had happened. But instead of reassuring Marcus, this only deepened his uneasy fears.

He left the drawing room, and found Penelope standing in the hallway outside the small parlor. She appeared lost in thought, and as he approached he saw that her face was pale and drawn.

"Is there anything wrong?" he asked.

"No, why would there be?"

"The footman John came to get you," Marcus said. "You left the room, and when you did not return I grew concerned."

"Of course. Mr. Campbell had a question about the wine. It was no great matter," Penelope said.

"And that was all?"

"Yes," Penelope said.

He felt his stomach clench. He knew she was lying. If Mr. Campbell had truly summoned her, she would have been gone only a moment or two, not the more than quarter hour that had passed. And there was nothing in such a request that would have upset her.

Nor would there have been any reason for Mr. Wolcott to follow her.

"Was there some reason you sought me out? Is there something you wanted?" Penelope asked.

Yes, he thought. *I want the truth. I want to know what is between you and Stephen Wolcott. I want to know who has hurt you and why you feel compelled to lie to me about it. I want to make you my wife in truth, and not just in name.* But now he wondered if that would ever be possible.

All these thoughts and more flashed through his mind in an instant. A part of him wanted to take her aside and demand that she answer his questions. But another part of him, the part that had been raised to do his duty as a gentleman, knew that this was neither the time nor the place for such a confrontation. They had a roomful of guests to attend to. There would be time later to sort this matter out.

"I was looking for you," he said. "Come now, our guests are waiting."

Penelope pasted a smile on her face, and he wondered if anyone beside himself could tell how false it was. And then she took his arm and allowed him to lead her back to the party.

Somehow he managed to endure the remaining hours until the last of the guests took their leave. Unaccustomed to city hours, he was nearly stumbling with fatigue when he and Penelope sought their beds, and too exhausted to make more than a token protest when Penelope retired to her own bedchamber. It was for the best, he tried to tell himself, as he crawled into his cold and solitary bed. He was too tired for tact, and if Penelope had joined him, he would not have been able to hold back the accusations that had simmered in the back of his mind all evening. Far better to face her when they both had their wits about them.

But the next morning Penelope sent word through a maid that she was too unwell to join him at breakfast. He suspected her of trying to avoid him, but when he scratched at her bedroom door and entered, he found that she did indeed look unwell, her brow dotted with fatigue, and her hazel eyes appearing huge in her pale visage. Ashamed of his suspicions, Marcus simply bade her rest and wished her a speedy recovery. He spent the day quietly about his own pursuits.

Penelope did not join him for dinner that evening. Nor did he see her the next morning, although when he stopped by to check on her, he found that she had been well enough to dress and leave the house, although no one seemed to know her destination or when she would return.

It could mean nothing. Penelope could have left the house for any number of reasons. A trip to the library, a fitting at the dressmaker's, or even to call on one of her many friends. There were a hundred innocent reasons why she might have gone out.

But if her destination had been innocent, then there was no reason why she wouldn't have told him, or left word with the servants when to expect her return. Especially not when she had spent the last two days avoiding his company, claiming she was too unwell to see him.

There was one other explanation that came to mind. Penelope was avoiding him out of guilt. Even now, his wife might be dallying with her lover. One part of him rejected the idea immediately, but another part, the part that had wondered what she could possibly see in him, that part found all too much evidence to support his conjecture. He felt physically ill at the thought that Penelope might have allowed another man to touch her. He was furious. He was hurt beyond all measure. He wanted to yell. He wanted to break something. He wanted to be gone from here and never see her again except on formal occasions. He wanted it not to be true. He wanted to turn back the clock, and start all over again.

He did not know what he wanted. What he needed was the truth. And that only Penelope could provide.

Marcus sent for her personal maid, but Jenna was nowhere to be found. One footman thought that the maid might have accompanied Penelope, while another seemed to remember that Jenna had left on her own errand, sometime before her mistress. In either case, he would have to wait until either Penelope or her maid returned to learn more.

An hour passed, and then another. It was after noon when Marcus found at least some of the answers he sought, in the person of Mr. Stephen Wolcott.

Marcus had been surprised when Mr. Campbell informed him of the identity of his caller. After a moment's consideration he directed that Mr. Wolcott be shown into the small library, and there Marcus joined him.

"Your Grace, I hope you will forgive my presumption in coming here unannounced. I promise I will only take a moment of your time," Mr. Wolcott said.

Marcus found himself at a loss. He had spent the past hours trying not to imagine Penelope lost in another gentleman's embrace, only to be confronted by the very man he suspected of seducing his wife. Looking at Mr. Wolcott, whose immaculate grooming could not hide his thinning hair or growing paunch, it was impossible to imagine him seducing anyone. Nor would he credit him with having the gall to bed a duchess in the morning and then call upon her husband in the afternoon.

Perhaps it had all been a product of his jealousy. Perhaps there was an innocent explanation, and when Penelope returned she would be able to set his mind at rest. Someday he would laugh at how he had allowed himself to be carried away by foolish imaginings. For the first time in hours he found himself beginning to hope.

"I can spare a few moments," Marcus said. "Although I am at a loss to know why you would want to see me. My wife is the scholar of our house, and she is presently not at home."

"I know Penelope is not here," Mr. Wolcott said. "For she is the reason I have come."

Marcus's world came crashing down. And perhaps the simplest explanation was the truth.

"Yes?" Marcus asked, affecting a bored tone. He leaned back in his seat, stretching his legs out in front of him.

"You may have noticed that Penelope and I

have a rather . . . warm friendship," Mr. Wolcott insinuated.

It made his skin crawl to hear this worm use Penelope's name.

"My wife has many friends," Marcus observed.

"But only one with whom she has become intimate. One who shares her special passions, as it were."

A red haze covered his vision. Marcus's fists clenched, giving lie to his pretense of unconcern. He wanted nothing more than to wipe the leering smirk from Stephen Wolcott's face with his fists. But he held his temper, waiting to see what else Mr. Wolcott would say.

"Others have noticed our closeness, as well," Stephen Wolcott continued. "It is only a matter of time before our connection is common knowledge. And then there will be no avoiding scandal."

"I do not believe you," Marcus said reflexively, clinging to the hope that Penelope had not betrayed him.

"What else did you expect?" Stephen asked. "Your wife is a beautiful woman, left on her own in the city. Of course it was only a matter of time before she took a lover. You are fortunate that I have been so discreet. And that I am willing to be accommodating."

Discreet? Accommodating? Was this man insane, implying that he had somehow been noble in his treatment of Penelope? Did he not realize that even now Marcus was holding on to his temper by only the barest of margins?

"Accommodating how?"

"For a small consideration, I would be willing to leave Scotland, and return to my travels. Say ten thousand pounds? A gift of patronage, as it were. With such a sum I could support myself for several years."

"Ten thousand pounds seems a high price to pay to avoid scandal," Marcus said. "You must think highly of yourself."

"On the contrary, it is quite cheap. Think of it as an investment in your family's future. After all, you don't want there to be any doubt about the legitimacy of your heir, do you?" He gave a knowing leer. "Truly I am being quite considerate. Penelope is so besotted with me that I am certain she would give me far more than ten thousand pounds in gifts, were I to stay in Edinburgh and enjoy her friendship."

"She would do no such thing," Marcus countered, for the sake of arguing.

"I see you know little of her character," Stephen said. "Really, what else did you expect? Only a lightskirt would have answered that lunatic advertisement of yours. She always had her eye on the main chance. If it was not me, it would have been someone else."

Marcus's restless hands stilled, and he looked down at the floor. Mr. Wolcott's words echoed in his mind. He looked up, feeling a smile break across his face.

"On the contrary, it is you who have demonstrated your ignorance of my wife," Marcus said. "In every way."

Mr. Wolcott had made a fatal error. He had been halfway to convincing Marcus of Penelope's guilt, his sly insinuations fed on by Marcus's own guilty suspicions. But there was one thing that Mr. Wolcott did not know. Penelope had not written in answer to the advertisement. Indeed, Marcus had been the one to persuade her into this marriage.

He did not know what Mr. Wolcott's game was, but he was damned if he was going to play along.

"I believe our business is concluded," Marcus said, rising to his feet.

Mr. Wolcott rose as well. "And our arrangement?"

"There is no arrangement," Marcus said. "I will not dignify your slander. You may count yourself lucky that I allow you to take your leave. Should you ever call on this house again, poet or not, I will call you out."

"You will regret this," Mr. Wolcott said. "I will cause such a scandal that it will ruin you and your wife."

Marcus shook his head. "I advise you to think very carefully before you do anything rash," he said, allowing all of his pent-up anger to seep into his tone. "Do not mistake me for one of your literary set. I am a man of deeds, not of words. Threaten me or my wife again, and I will make you suffer. Is that understood?"

Mr. Wolcott paled as Marcus stepped closer, allowing his sheer physical bulk to intimidate the smaller man. It gave a brief satisfaction. Beating Mr. Wolcott to a bloody pulp would be more satisfying, but doing so in his own library would undoubtedly lead to just the sort of scandal that Marcus was trying to avoid.

"Is that understood?" Marcus repeated.

"Yes," Mr. Wolcott hissed, turning on his heel and stalking from the room.

Marcus watched him go with a sense of satisfaction. He owed Penelope the chance to make her own explanations for her behavior. He would trust in her to tell him the truth.

SIXTEEN

Penelope's heart was heavy as she returned to the house at Charlotte Square. She handed her wrap to the waiting footman, and untied the strings to her bonnet.

"Lord Torringford wishes to speak with you, at your convenience," the footman said.

"I will see him at once," Penelope said. Postponing their discussion would only give her more time to fret. "Is my husband in his study?"

"I believe he is in the library," the footman said.

"Then I will meet him there. Oh, and has my maid Jenna returned?"

"Yes, some time ago."

Jenna had accompanied her as she called upon Mr. Wolcott. It had made her skin crawl to see him again, but she dared not put her answer in a letter, which he might later try to use against her.

Their encounter had been brief and acrimonious. Penelope had flatly refused to pay the blackmail he demanded, insisting that her innocence was the only protection she needed. She mocked his threats, reminding him that she and Marcus had already survived one great scandal, and that there were few who would give credence to any tales he might care to spread.

It had been a brave performance, but after she left his rooms, Penelope had begun to shake. Her brave words had masked the real fear she felt inside. Mr. Wolcott could indeed blacken her name, if he tried. After all, she had given him plenty of ammunition by allowing him to appear so frequently as her escort. But it was not the blackening of her name she feared, so much as it was the damage his accusations could do to her marriage.

She had even thought about giving in, and paying the money he demanded, though she had no idea how on earth she would obtain such a sum. But after a long and sleepless night she had rejected the idea. She knew better than to suppose that five thousand pounds represented the sum of his ambitions. If she gave him the money now, he would return again and again, until he bled her dry.

And if Marcus ever discovered that she had paid blackmail, it would seem confirmation of her guilt.

Jenna had waited outside as Penelope met with Mr. Wolcott. Her presence was a comfort, even though the maid could not hear the conversation; still, bringing her there paid at least lip service to the forms of propriety.

After meeting with Mr. Wolcott, she had sent Jenna home. There was one more person she needed to speak with, and for this encounter she wanted no witnesses. And indeed the doctor confirmed what she had suspected for these past weeks, and now she had another dilemma. How ever was she to break the news to Marcus? Her timing could not possibly be any worse.

The footman cleared his throat, and Penelope gave a startled jump as she realized she had been standing in the entryway, lost in her thoughts.

"Thank you," she said, dismissing him.

She made her way to the library, and found Marcus pacing back and forth on the small carpet before the unlit fireplace. As he glanced at her, she realized that he looked weary, almost as weary as she herself felt.

"Are you feeling better?" he asked.

"Yes, thank you," Penelope said. "Well enough that I needed to take care of some errands that would brook no delay."

"Please, take a seat," Marcus said. "You still do not look well. I do not think it was wise for you to be up and about today."

Penelope sank down on a padded chair. Marcus took his seat directly across from her, pinning her with his gaze.

She took a deep breath and gathered her courage, realizing that the time had come for her to speak.

"I fear I have been most unwise," Penelope began. "And I need you to hear me out before you pass judgment."

Marcus nodded gravely. "I am listening."

Penelope clasped her hands in her lap. "I believe I told you when we first met that as a girl of sixteen I had once been in love? Or at least back then I thought it was love."

Now she knew it had not been love. It had been nothing but a foolish infatuation on her part. But knowing such did not assuage the hurt.

"In my youthful folly I might have indeed ruined myself. But my father, far wiser than I, made arrangements for the gentleman to disappear from my life. He paid him to leave Edinburgh. The gentleman was Stephen Wolcott."

"I see," Marcus said. His tone was even, but he would not look her in the eye.

"I never knew what my father had done," Penelope said. "I spent years convinced that I had lost my own chance for true love, and then Mr. Wolcott reappeared."

"You discovered you were still in love with him," Marcus said in a low voice.

"No, I knew there could be nothing between us but friendship. That is what I wanted, and what I thought he wanted as well. But it seems he wanted more."

"He wanted to be your lover."

If only it had been that simple. But Stephen Wolcott's passions had been far colder.

"He wanted my money. Or, rather, your money," Penelope explained, looking at the patterned carpet as she revealed the full extent of her humiliation. She could not bear to look at Marcus. Could not bear to see either condemnation or sympathy in his gaze.

"He was not particular about how he got it. When I told him we could be no more than friends, he tried to blackmail me. Said that he would tell you we had had an affair, unless I gave him five thousand pounds. Naturally I refused. But I am afraid that he is not done making trouble. I do not know what to do, and so I need your help."

"Today his price is ten thousand pounds," Marcus said slowly.

Her eyes flew up to his face. "What? What do you mean?"

Marcus nodded. "He came here today, demanding such a sum, or else he would go public with the scandal."

She swallowed hard, tasting bile. Stephen Wolcott had been here. He had already poisoned Marcus's ears with his lies. The very thing she had feared most had come to pass.

"And what did you tell him?" she asked. She was almost afraid to know. Afraid to find out that Marcus, like her father, had not trusted in her virtue. Had chosen instead to pay off the rogue, to protect what was left of her reputation.

"I told him to go hang," Marcus said.

"Truly?"

"Truly. I knew his accusations were false."

"But how? How did you know he was false? Even I was tricked by him. Twice."

"I will admit his words made me angry," Marcus said. "And I was jealous. But then I realized that he did not know you. Not the way that I do. And that while you may have bestowed your friendship unwisely, you would not betray your husband."

"I did not betray you," Penelope said. It was important that he know this. "There was nothing between us, except the foolish kisses I gave him as a young woman."

"I believe you," Marcus said.

She searched his face. He looked weary, but the grimness had left his expression.

"So what do we do now?" she asked.

Marcus rose, and crossed over to sit beside her on the sofa, taking her hand in his. She took comfort in his nearness, remembering the closeness that they had once shared. Perhaps it was not too late to find that closeness again.

His thumb idly traced the back of her hand. "What shall we do? As for this Mr. Wolcott, we will ignore him. I have already warned him. Should he try to make trouble, I can deal with such as he."

If Marcus stood by her, then there was hope they could escape this mess unscathed. If Penelope and Marcus showed a united front, then Mr. Wolcott's lies would be seen as no more than scurrilous slander, and swiftly forgotten.

"And what about us?" Penelope asked. "Shall you go back to Greenfields once this is over?"

"What do you want?" Marcus asked.

It was time to speak her heart. She should have done so weeks ago, when they first returned to Edinburgh. Instead she had kept her silence, assuming that Marcus still planned to hold to the original terms of their agreement. A marriage of convenience, no more.

She had been a coward, and she had paid the price, for Marcus had returned to Greenfields, leaving her alone in Edinburgh. Where, in her misery, she had allowed herself to be led into folly.

Now she said what she should have said all those weeks ago.

"I want to be with you. Here, at the Abbey, or even at Greenfields, if you will take me there." Penelope bit her lip, then added, "There is one blessing to come from this affair. I realized that I am indeed in love with you."

Marcus squeezed her hand. "I, too, have a confession to make," he said. "I lied about my reasons for coming to Edinburgh. I came here because I missed you. Because I realized I love you. I do not want you to be my duchess, I want you to be my wife."

Moments ago she had been in black despair, and now she felt an upwelling of joy within her. Marcus loved her. It was impossible. It was glorious. It was everything she had wanted, and had thought that she had lost forever through her folly.

"Yes," she said, as her face split in a foolish smile.

Marcus leaned forward, and kissed her. She wrapped her arms around him, cherishing the feeling of his body pressed against hers, as he claimed her with his lips, the warmth of his passion washing away her fears.

"Come home with me," Marcus said.

"Yes," Penelope replied. "Our child should be born in the country."

Marcus drew back a moment. "Our child?"

Penelope nodded. "I saw Dr. Harris this morning. It seems we will always have a reminder of those days at Torringford Abbey. I will have a child before the springtime."

"A son," Marcus breathed.

"Or a daughter," Penelope said.

"Let us hope she has your beauty," Marcus said.

"And her father's sense of honor," Penelope replied.

EPILOGUE

The June sun shone brilliantly overhead as Reginald Heywood rode into the stableyard of Torringford Abbey. As he dismounted, he heard his name called out, and looked over to see his brother Marcus emerging from the main house.

"Reginald," his brother called again, striding across the cobblestones and embracing him. "I did not expect you until tomorrow at the earliest."

Reginald returned the embrace, and then stepped back. There were faint creases of tiredness around Marcus's eyes, but his face was relaxed, and his smile open and unguarded. Marcus looked happy, he realized. Far happier than he could ever remember seeing him in these many years since their parents' deaths.

"The weather was fine, and I could not wait to see you," Reginald said. "And my new niece and nephew. They are well, I trust?"

"They are perfect. In every way," Marcus said. "I stopped in Edinburgh on my journey, and there is a package of correspondence for you from McGregor," Reginald said, nodding toward his saddlebags. "Plus I must tell you of the new works at Greenfields, and get your advice."

Marcus shrugged. "That can wait. Come, you must see the children for yourself. Penelope and the nurse have brought them out to enjoy the fine day."

Reginald followed Marcus through the stable yard, past the small kitchen garden, and onto the south lawn. They paused as they rounded the corner, Marcus's eyes drinking in the sight before him.

Colorful blankets had been spread on the grass, and on them sat Penelope and a young woman who must be the nursery maid. Each held a rosy-cheeked baby in their lap, while Princess, the beagle who had adopted Penelope, sat nearby, jealously guarding her mistress.

"They look very fine, do they not?" Marcus asked.

"They look beautiful," Reginald said, feeling a sudden pang of envy. He did not begrudge Marcus the fortune and title he had inherited, but indeed he envied him his happiness. For it was clear that Marcus had found everything he wanted, in the company of his new wife and children. No wonder he wore the look of contentment.

Indeed, after that first summer, Marcus and Penelope had come to a new understanding, as they realized that they had fallen in love with each other. Marcus had generously given Greenfields over to Reginald, and he and Penelope made Torringford Abbey their home. They still visited Edinburgh from time to time, and talked of going to London next Season. But it was clear that it was here that Marcus's heart lay.

Just then Penelope caught sight of them and waved, her face breaking into a happy smile. As Marcus smiled back in return, Reginald realized that his brother was a lucky man indeed.

"To think that a year ago, when I learned of the old duke's will, I pitied you," Reginald said as they began crossing the lawn. "And then when the advertisement appeared, I felt ashamed for having added to your trials."

"And now?"

"Now I think Greenfields is only fair recompense for the happiness my meddling has brought you," Reginald teased.

Marcus grinned. "Indeed I am in your debt. We both are."

"Reginald, what a wonderful surprise. And see, this is your niece Anna Caroline," Penelope said, holding up the infant in her arms. "And this is your nephew, Thomas Reginald James, the Earl of Knox. They are four weeks old today."

"I am pleased to make their acquaintance," Reginald said, bowing gravely before taking a seat on the blanket. "I am no expert, but they are very fine babies indeed."

Indeed, the small blanket-wrapped babes looked much like any other babies he had seen.

Though, from the besotted expression on Marcus's and Penelope's faces, it was clear that their parents thought that the twins were extraordinary.

Reginald duly admired the children, and assured Penelope that she was even more beautiful than she had been before the marriage. Somewhat doubtfully he accepted the squirming bundle that was his niece and held her in his lap, as she drooled prettily upon his new waistcoat. Fortunately Penelope rescued him before the infant could do more damage.

"Yes, I think things turned out very well indeed," Reginald observed, as he handed Anna Caroline back to her mother. "Perhaps I should consider placing my own advertisement for a wife."

"No!" Marcus and Penelope said in unison.

He grinned at their obvious chagrin. "It was only a jest. I promise that I have reformed. Truly," he said.

"Good. For I'd hate to have to advertise for a new brother," Marcus said.

More Zebra Regency Romances

Stella Cameron

"A premier author of romantic suspense."

__The Best Revenge
0-8217-5842-X $6.50US/$8.00CAN

__French Quarter
0-8217-6251-6 $6.99US/$8.50CAN

__Key West
0-8217-6595-7 $6.99US/$8.99CAN

__Pure Delights
0-8217-4798-3 $5.99US/$6.99CAN

__Sheer Pleasures
0-8217-5093-3 $5.99US/$6.99CAN

__True Bliss
0-8217-5369-X $5.99US/$6.99CAN

The Queen of
Romance

Cassie Edwards

Discover The Magic of Romance With

Jo Goodman